Brother Cadfael's
Book of Days

Cadfael books by Robin Whiteman

Cadfael Country
The Cadfael Companion
Brother Cadfael's Herb Garden

Other books by Robin Whiteman (with Rob Talbot)

ENGLISH LANDSCAPES
LAKELAND LANDSCAPES
YORKSHIRE LANDSCAPES
COTSWOLD LANDSCAPES
ENGLAND
THE COTSWOLDS
THE ENGLISH LAKES
THE YORKSHIRE MOORS & DALES
THE HEART OF ENGLAND
THE WEST COUNTRY
WESSEX
THE GARDEN OF ENGLAND
EAST ANGLIA & THE FENS
THE PEAK DISTRICT
NORTHUMBRIA
SHAKESPEARE'S AVON

Web site
www.talbot-whiteman.freeserve.co.uk

Brother Cadfael's Book of Days

Robin Whiteman

BASED ON THE

Cadfael Chronicles

BY

Ellis Peters

HEADLINE

First published in Great Britain in 2000 by
HEADLINE BOOK PUBLISHING

1 3 5 7 9 10 8 6 4 2

British Library Cataloguing in Publication Data
Brother Cadfael's book of days: the material and spiritual
wisdom of a medieval crusader-monk
I. Cadfael, Brother (Fictitious character) – Quotations, maxims, etc.
I. Whiteman, Robin, 1944– II. Peters, Ellis, 1913–1995
823.9 14

ISBN 0 7472 6477 5
Printed and bound in Great Britain by
Mackays of Chatham, PLC, Chatham, Kent

HEADLINE BOOK PUBLISHING
A division of Hodder Headline
338 Euston Road
London NW1 3BH

www.headline.co.uk
www.hodderheadline.com

Contents

Introduction

The Cadfael Chronicles by Ellis Peters (whose real name was Edith Pargeter) are not simply well-written and meticulously researched medieval detective mysteries – they are modern morality tales, exploring the whole range of human experience, material and spiritual: life and death, love and hate, hope and despair, good and evil . . . Yet common sense, justice, truth, compassion and forgiveness triumph in the end.

Skilfully woven into the unfolding narrative of each of the twenty Chronicles (and, therefore, often overlooked) is a wealth of jewel-like wisdom, culled from a long lifetime, rich with experience – a wisdom that acknowledges shadow and light, heaven and hell, human frailty and spiritual strength.

Although the Chronicles are set in the medieval period, Edith Pargeter was very much a woman of her time; she may have written vividly about the past, but she was passionately aware of the present. In addition to writing fictional and historical novels, she also wrote about contemporary issues (including her wartime experiences), translated works from Czech into English, and – among many honours received – was awarded an OBE in 1994 (the year before her death) 'for services to literature'.

It is not surprising, therefore, that many who have read, and reread, the Cadfael Chronicles have discovered meaning, relevance and inspiration in Edith's words. For among the wide-ranging thoughts, words and deeds of her fictional medieval crusader-monk there is much to meditate on, much to heed, and much that is relevant for the world today.

For those who may not have heard of Brother Cadfael, let alone read any of the Cadfael Chronicles, there follow a few facts that may prove useful.

Cadfael was born in North Wales in May 1080. At the age of fourteen he went to Shrewsbury, on the English side of the Welsh border, and entered the service of a wool merchant. In 1097, despite falling in love with a local girl, he left England to go on crusade to the Holy Land. After half a lifetime of roving, fighting, loving and accumulating wisdom (including knowledge of herbs), Cadfael returned to England in 1120. He entered the Benedictine abbey at Shrewsbury as a novice and, over the years, worked hard to create one of the finest monastic herb-gardens in the land. From soldier, sailor and crusader, therefore, he became a monk, herbalist and apothecary and, of course, champion of justice and solver of crimes and mysteries.

It was within his workshop, in the herb garden at Shrewsbury Abbey, that Cadfael brewed his medicines, did his best thinking and shared many a pleasant hour, talking and drinking, with his friend Hugh Beringar, sheriff of Shrewsbury.

Mention should also be made of Saint Winifred, the Welsh saint who held a special place in Cadfael's heart. After all, he had openly taken her bones out of her grave in Gwytherin and then secretly put them back again. Unknowingly, his brother monks had taken back to Shrewsbury a reliquary containing a body other than that of the saint – a deception for which Saint Winifred readily forgave Cadfael. He often addressed her in Welsh, 'but usually he relied on her to know all the preoccupations of his mind without words'. It should also be noted that Cadfael lived in a relatively uncomplicated 'Age of Faith', where miracles were not only possible, they were assured through grace.

The Cadfael Chronicles are, in fact, a skilful blend of fact and fiction. The first novel is set in the spring of 1137, the second in the summer of 1138. Thereafter, they progress season by season, year by year, until December 1145, when the final novel ends. During this period, England was racked by a long fratricidal civil war, fought between the supporters of King Stephen and those of his cousin the Empress Maud. It started when Stephen seized the throne in 1135 and ended in 1153, when he signed a treaty designating Henry Plantagenet (Maud's son) as his successor. After Stephen's death the following year, Henry was crowned King Henry II.

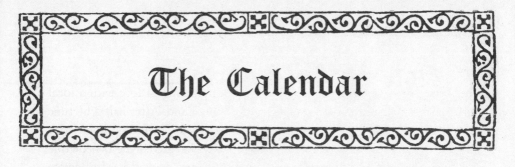

The Calendar

In the old Roman calendar – supposedly created in the eighth century BC by Romulus, the legendary founder of Rome – the year began in March and consisted of ten months, totalling 304 days. Romulus's successor, Numa Pompilius, is credited with adding two more months, January and February, bringing the number of days in a year to 355.

The Julian calendar of twelve months and 365 days (with a leap year of 366 days every fourth year) was introduced in the mid first century BC by Julius Caesar. This purely solar calendar replaced the previous, basically lunar calendar. Caesar also made January, rather than March, the first month of the year (a reform introduced at least a century earlier, with only partial success).

Nevertheless, during the Middle Ages – despite the widespread adoption of the Julian calendar – there was no consensus amongst Europeans as to when the year began: some localities, for example, observed New Year's Day on 25 December; others celebrated it on 1 January; and yet others maintained it was on or around Easter. In Britain the year started on 25 March. In 1582, when the Gregorian calendar (also called the Christian or New Style calendar) was introduced by Pope Gregory XIII, Roman Catholic countries started to observe New Year's Day on 1 January. Although Scotland followed suit relatively quickly, it was not until 1752 that England finally adopted the Gregorian calendar and, by order of Parliament, moved New Year's Day from 25 March to 1 January.

Brother Cadfael's Book of Days, like the Cadfael Chronicles, begins the new year on 1 January. Spring starts on 21 March (about the vernal equinox); summer on 21 June (about the summer solstice); autumn on 21 September (about the autumnal equinox); and winter on 21 December (about the winter solstice).

Note on the Source Material

The source material, more often than not, forms an integral part of the narrative of each of the Cadfael Chronicles.

To enable each extract to exist independently of the novels, it has been necessary, on occasions, to make alterations to the original text, whilst preserving the original meaning.

The extracts, therefore, may not *exactly* match the words found in the Cadfael Chronicles. But, rest assured, they do remain true to the spirit of Brother Cadfael and, more importantly, to the thoughts and beliefs of his creator Ellis Peters (Edith Pargeter).

The reference at the end of each extract refers to the chronicle and chapter: 7(4), therefore, means Chronicle 7 (Chapter 4). Chronicle 4, however, has five parts, each subdivided into 'chapters'. Chronicle 4(4:4), then, means Chronicle 4 (Part 4, Chapter 4).

The Cadfael Chronicles
by Ellis Peters

Published by Little Brown (1–13) and Headline (14–20) in hardback;
and Headline in trade paperback (14–20), and Warner Futura in paperback (1–20).

A Rare Benedictine, 1988

(A collection of short stories published by Headline)

January

The first day of the New Year dawned grey and moist, but with a veiled light that suggested the sun might come through slowly, and abide for an hour or so in the middle of the day. 12(11)

January

1st You can fairly claim the day hasn't been wasted, if something's been learned. 1(4)

✻❈✻

2nd Thank God I didn't make the mistake of suggesting it to him. There's nothing the young hate and resent so much as to be urged to a good act, when they've already made the virtuous resolve on their own account. 3(11)

✻❈✻

3rd It is a matter of values. Study to learn what is worth and what is not, and you may come to understand. 10(14)

January

4th The day will come when all will be made plain. Then shall we
know, as now we trust. 12(11)

❧❖❧

5th In no times, good or bad, can man do more or better than
choose his own road according to his conscience, and bear the
consequences of his choice, whatever they may be. 2(7)

❧❖❧

6th If you have not found it, you cannot *know* where it is, you
can only surmise, which is not the same thing. 3(5)

January

7th There was a little while yet to wait before Matins began at the midnight hour, the celebration of God made flesh, virgin-born and wonderful. Why should not the Holy Spirit engender, as fire kindles fire and light, the necessary instrument of flesh no more than the fuel that renders its substance to provide warmth and enlightenment? He who questions has already denied himself any answer.

12(4)

8th I do not deny divine grace. The grace is in the gifts he has given us, free will to choose good and refuse evil, and mount towards our own salvation, yes, and the strength to choose rightly. If we do our part, God will do the rest.

16(5)

9th There is a right place for every soul under the sun.

8(6)

January

10th Despair is deadly sin, but worse it is mortal folly. God is looking your way as attentively as ever he did. And all you have to do to deserve is to wait in patience, and keep up your heart.

8(6)

⁂

11th In happiness or unhappiness, living is a duty, and must be done thoroughly.

13(1)

⁂

12th Violence can never be anything but ugly, but we live in a world as ugly and violent as it is beautiful and good. 4(4:4)

January

13th Cadfael discerned a deep and tranquil satisfaction in the shepherd's life. Shepherds had a community of their own, peopled with gentle, obstinate, quiet companions, who did no murder or theft or banditry, broke no laws, made no complaints, fuelled no rebellions. All the same, he thought, I could not be a shepherd for long. I should miss all the things I deplore, the range and grasp of man for good and evil. And instantly he was back with the struggles and victories and victims of the day. 3(9)

14th What is gone may return. The roads lead always two ways, hither as well as yonder. 10(12)

January

15th Cadfael forbore from citing his own travels, remembered now with the astonished contentment of a man at rest. To tell the truth, he enjoyed the storms no less than he now enjoyed the calm: but each had its own time and place. 3(9)

16th He had seen battles, in his time in the world, and witnessed deaths crueller than disease, and heathen kinder than Christians, and he knew of leprosies of the heart and ulcers of the soul worse than any of these he poulticed and lanced with his herbal medicines. 5(1)

17th A blind eye is the easiest thing in the world to turn on whatever is troublesome. 3(1)

January

18th England was already frozen into a winter years long, the king was crowned, and held, however slackly, most of England. The empress, his rival for the throne, held the west, and came with a claim the equal of his. Cousins, most uncousinly, they tore each other and tore England between them, and yet life must go on, faith must go on, the stubborn defiance of fortune must go on in the husbandry of the year, season after season, plough and harrow and seed, tillage and harvest. And here in the cloister and the church, the sowing and tillage and harvest of souls. Brother Cadfael had no fear for mankind, whatever became of mere men. The birth of his friend's child would be a new generation, a new beginning, a new affirmation, spring in midwinter.

6(1)

After the death of his uncle, Henry I, in 1135, Stephen of Blois seized the throne of England and had himself crowned king at Westminster. His action heralded the start of a long fratricidal civil war — between himself and his cousin, the Empress Maud (the dead king's daughter and only legitimate heir) — which lasted for almost all of Stephen's troubled reign.

Cadfael's friend was, of course, Hugh Beringar, sheriff of Shrewsbury. Hugh's child, Giles, was born in 1139.

January

19th When the king is all too busy in the south, and his mind on where his army's next pay is to come from, and his energy mostly wasted in wavering from one target to another, ambitious men in remoter parts are liable to begin to spread their honours into palatines, and set up kingdoms of their own. And given the example, the lesser fry will follow it. $6(1)$

20th All the border towns were at risk, as well from the precarious loyalties of constables and garrisons as from the enterprise of the enemy. More than one lord in this troubled land had already changed his allegiance, more than one would do so in the future, some, perhaps, for the second or third time. Churchmen, barons and all, they were beginning to look first to their own interests, and place their loyalty where it seemed likely to bring them the greater profit. And it would not be long before some of them came to the conclusion that their interests could be served just as well by flouting both contendants for the crown, and setting up on their own account. $6(1)$

January

21^{**st**} 'This has become a war which cannot be won or lost. Victory and defeat have become alike impossible. Unfortunately it may take several years yet before most men begin to understand.'

'If there is no winning and no losing, there has to be another way. No land can continue for ever in a chaotic stalemate between two exhausted forces, without governance, while two groups of bewildered old men squat on their meagre gains and stare helplessly at each other, unable to lift a hand for the *coup de grâce*.'

'It has gone on too long, and it will go on some years yet. But there is no ending that way, except by the death of all the old men, from stagnation and old age and disgust. I would rather not wait to make one of them.'

'Nor I! And therefore, what does a sane man do while he's enduring such waiting as he can endure?'

'Tills his own ground, shepherds his own flock, mends his own fences, and sharpens his own sword.'

'Collects his own revenues? And pays his own dues?'

'Both. To the last penny. And his own counsel. Even while the terms like traitor and turncoat are being bandied about like arrows finding random marks.'

19(II)

In 1145 Robert de Beaumont, Earl of Leicester, and Hugh Beringar, sheriff of Shrewsbury, discussed, in wary confidence, the ruinous state of the realm. Despite adopting an attitude of neutrality, the earl remained loyal to King Stephen — only transferring his allegiance to the empress and her son, Henry Plantagenet, in 1153.

January

22nd There was, Cadfael could not but admit, room for a little hard practicality within the abbey walls, if the truth were told. The abbot of late had grown deeply discouraged with the world of men, and withdrawn more and more into his prayers. The siege and fall of Shrewsbury, with all the bloodshed and revenge involved, had been enough to sadden any man, though that was no excuse for abandoning the effort to defend right and oppose wrong. But there comes a time when the old grow very tired, and the load of leadership unjustly heavy to bear. And perhaps — perhaps! — the abbot would not be quite so sad as even he now supposed, if the load should be lifted from him. 3(1)

Appointed abbot of Shrewsbury Abbey in 1127, Heribert was slow to support King Stephen during his siege of the castle in 1138. He was subsequently stripped of his office, and spent the remaining years of his life as a simple choir-monk — freed of heavy burden and pleasantly content.

23rd Wonderful what riches a man can bestow who by choice and vocation possesses nothing! The world is full of small, beneficent miracles. 18(1)

January

24th 'I grow herbs,' said Brother Cadfael, 'and dry them, and make remedies for all the ills that visit us. I physic a great many souls besides those of us within.'

'And that satisfies you?' It would not have satisfied him.

'To heal men, after years of injuring them? What could be more fitting? A man does what he must do,' said Cadfael carefully, 'whether the duty he has taken on himself is to fight, or to salvage poor souls from the fighting, to kill, to die or to heal. There are many will claim to tell you what is due from you, but only one who can shear through the many, and reach the truth. And that is you, by what light falls for you to show the way.' 8(2)

Cadfael was talking to Meriet Aspley, who had been forced, by his father, to enter Shrewsbury Abbey as a novice. Because his tormented dreams disturbed the sleep of the other novices, Meriet was accused of bringing a demon into the monastery with him — he was therefore known as the 'Devil's Novice'.

25th God's mercy is infinite to those who seek it, however late, however feebly. 7(13)

January

26th People, thought Cadfael, people are endlessly mysterious, and I am endlessly curious. A sin to be confessed, no doubt, and well worth a penance. As long as man is curious about his fellow man, that appetite alone will keep him alive.   10(6)

27th 'Oh, I know the weight of the case you can make against this boy,' said Cadfael. 'I could make as good a case against one or two more, but that I won't do. I'd rather by far consider those factors that might provide, not suspicion, but proof, and not against one chosen quarry, but against the person, whoever he may be, towards whom the facts point.'   3(5)

28th He rose like one in a dream, both spent and renewed, as though some rainfall from heaven had washed him out of his agony and out of his wits, to revive, a man half-drowned and wholly transformed.   3(1)

January

29th Strange chances do jostle one another sometimes in this world. Don't put it clean out of mind, it may still be true.

4(2:3)

***

30th Well, they happen, the lightning-strokes of God, the gifted or misfortunates who are born into a world where they nowhere belong, the saints and scholars who come to manhood unrecognised, guarding the swine in the forest pastures among the beech-mast, the warrior princes villein-born and youngest in a starving clan, set to scare the crows away from the furrow. Just as hollow slave-rearlings are cradled in the palaces of kings, and come to rule, however ineptly, over men a thousand times their worth.

6(8)

January

31^{**st**} A curious theme intruded itself into Cadfael's musings. This matter of the occasional guests of the abbey, so-called, the souls who chose to abandon the working world, sometimes in their prime, and hand over their inheritance to the abbey for a soft, shielded, inactive life in a house of retirement, with food, clothing, firing, all provided without the lifting of a finger! Did they dream of it for years? A little sub-paradise where meals dropped from the sky and there was nothing to do but bask, in the summer, and toast by the fire with mulled ale in the winter? And when they got to it, how long did the enchantment last? How soon did they sicken of doing nothing, and needing to do nothing? In a man blind, lame, sick, he could understand the act. But in those hale and busy, and used to exerting body and mind? No, that he could not understand. There must be other motives. Not all men could be deceived, or deceive themselves, into mistaking idleness for blessedness. 3(1)

After falling out with his stepson, sixty-year-old Gervase Bonel,
Lord of Mallilie, decided to cut him off without a penny and grant his
inheritance to Shrewsbury Abbey. In return, the abbey agreed to feed,
clothe and house Bonel for the rest of his life.

February

※※◈※※

There were occasional spells of frost, but none that lasted long, and such snow-showers as there were were fitful and slight, but did not lie long. 15(3)

February

1ˢᵗ Those who go forth to the battle never return without holes in their ranks, like gaping wounds. Pity of all pities that those who lead never learn, and the few wise men among those who follow never quite avail to teach. But faith given and allegiance pledged are stronger than fear, and that, perhaps, is virtue, even in the teeth of death.

9(1)

2ⁿᵈ If you ask for nothing, you deserve nothing.

9(15)

3ʳᵈ A man can but hold fast to what he believes right, and even the opponent he baulks should value him for that.

1(3)

February

4th 'You want to pay in full,' said Cadfael. 'Pay, then! Yours is a lifelong penance, I rule that you shall live out your life – and may it be long! – and pay back all your debts by having regard to those who inhabit this world with you. The tale of your good may yet outweigh a thousand times the tale of your evil. This is the penance I lay on you. 3(10)

After Cadfael had accused him of murder by poison, Meurig confronted the monk at knife-point. However, instead of killing him, he laid his life in Cadfael's hands.

5th Penance in confession, is the beginning of wisdom. Whatever grace can do, it cannot follow denial. 19(10)

6th What you do and what you are is what matters. 2(2)

February

7th On that day, which was the seventh of February of the year of our Lord 1141, they had offered special prayers at every office, not for the victory of one party or the defeat of another in the battlefields of the north, but for better counsel, for reconciliation, for the sparing of blood-letting and the respect of life between men of the same country — all desirable consummations, but very unlikely to be answered in this torn and fragmented land with any but a very dusty answer. Even God needs some consideration and support from his material to make reasoning and benign creatures of men.   9(1)

In early 1141 King Stephen marched north with his army to retake Lincoln Castle, which had been seized by Ranulf, Earl of Chester, and his half-brother, William of Roumare. During the ensuing battle — fought on 2 February — the king himself was captured. He was subsequently taken to Bristol and imprisoned in the castle.

8th Reverses are sent to us so that we may overcome them, and no man can presume to escape such testings for ever. The loss can be borne.   14(3)

9th Know you are not alone.   3(4)

February

10th 'Cadfael, do you know that you are speaking of that reliquary as if it truly contained Saint Winifred's bones. "She", you say, never "it", or even more truly "him". And you know, none so well, that you left her to her rest there in Wales. Can she be in two places at once?'

'Some essence of her certainly can,' said Cadfael, 'for she has done miracles here among us. She lay in that coffin three days, why should she not have conferred the power of her grace upon it? Is she to be limited by time and place? I tell you, sometimes I wonder what would be found within there, if ever that lid was lifted. Though I own,' he added ruefully, 'I shall be praying devoutly that it never comes to the proof.'

'You had better. Imagine the uproar, if someone somewhere breaks those seals you repaired so neatly, and prises off the lid, to find the body of a young man about twenty-four, instead of the bones of a virgin saint. And mother-naked, at that! Your goose would be finely cooked!'   19(3)

In 1137 a party of monks from Shrewsbury, led by Prior Robert (and
including Brother Cadfael), journeyed to Wales to secure the bones of St Winifred
for the abbey. Unbeknown to the party, Brother Cadfael opened the reliquary
and replaced the saint's remains with the corpse of Brother Columbanus.
Her relics were reburied in Welsh soil. The reliquary was taken to
Shrewsbury and installed in the abbey church.

February

11th 'A truly strange story,' said the earl, having listened with flattering concentration to the prior's eloquent exposition of the whole history of Shrewsbury's tenure of Saint Winifred, from her triumphant translation from Wales to an altar in the abbey, and her inexplicable disappearance during the flood. 'For it seems that she was removed from her own altar without human agency — or at least you have found none. And she has already been known, you tell me, to work miracles. Is it possible that for some beneficent purpose of her own she may have transferred herself miraculously from the place where she was laid? Can she have seen fit to pursue some errand of blessing elsewhere? Or felt some disaffection to the place where she was?'

19(4)

During the flood of February 1145 — when the River Severn burst its banks and threatened to engulf Shrewsbury Abbey — the reliquary containing the supposed bones of St Winifred was moved to a safer place. During the confusion, an attempt was made to steal the reliquary and take it to a distant abbey. It was eventually retrieved at Huncote, near Leicester, and brought back to Shrewsbury.

February

12th 'I planned and did what I have already told you,' said the
holy thief. 'I felt that I was doing no wrong. I believed I was
instructed, and faithfully I obeyed.'

'We have your story,' said the abbot of Shrewsbury. 'We have a
saint who has made her way back to us by strange ways, and we have
those who have been friends to her on that journey, and may well
believe, as you believe, that the lady has been in control of her own
destiny, and choosing her own friends and her own dependants.'

19(6)

*The person who tried to steal the reliquary of St Winifred, for the 'future glory'
of his abbey, was Tutilo, the 'Holy Thief', a Benedictine novice at Ramsey Abbey.
When accused, he maintained that he was carrying out the will of the saint.*

13th In the choir it was always dim, a parable of the life of man,
a small, lighted space arched over by a vast shadowy dark-
ness, for even in darkness there are degrees of shadow.   12(11)

February

14th 'Instruct me, Cadfael. I am not in the counsels of bishops and archbishops. Just how is the ordinance of heaven to be interpreted in these *sortes Biblicae*? Oh, certainly I know the common practice of reading the future by opening the Evangel blindly, and laying a finger on the page, but what is this official use of it in consecrating a new bishop? Too late then, surely, to change him for a better if the word goes against him.'

'I have never been in attendance at such a consecration myself,' Cadfael said. 'The bishops keep it within the circle. I marvel how the results ever leak out, but they do. Or someone makes them up, of course. Too sharp to be true, I sometimes feel. But yes, they are taken just as the abbot said, and very solemnly, so I'm told. The book of the Gospels is laid on the shoulders of the newly chosen bishop, and opened at random, and a finger laid on the page, possibly by the archbishop or bishop who is officiating. Though, granted, he could be friend or enemy to the new man. I trust they play fair, but who knows? Bad or good, that line is the prognostic for the bishop's future ministry. Apt enough, sometimes. But much can be done with the interpretation.'

19(7)

According to some medieval historians, the sortes Biblicae — *the custom of reading the future by opening the Gospels — was used officially in the ceremony of the consecration of a bishop. Not all sortes were favourable, and not all prognostics were the result of divine intervention.*

February

15th I opened the Gospels, and I got my answer, and it set me thinking afresh and seeing clearly where I had formerly been blind. And how to account for it I do not know, unless indeed it was the saint who spoke. 19(10)

※·※

16th The thing about fear is that it is pointless. When need arises, fear is forgotten. 5(2)

※·※

17th He felt in his heart that it was sin, the sin of despair; not despair for himself, but despair of truth and justice and right, and the future of wretched mankind. 3(6)

February

18th There are as holy persons outside orders as ever there are in, and not to trifle with truth, as good men out of the Christian church as most I've met within it. In the Holy Land I've known Saracens I'd trust before the common run of the crusaders, men honourable, generous and courteous, who would have scorned to haggle and jostle for place and trade as some of our allies did. Meet every man as you find him, for we're all made the same under habit or robe or rags. Some better made than others, and some better cared for, but on the same pattern all.   1(6)

❁◇❁

19th And God forgive me the lie, and turn it to truth. Or at least count it as merit to me rather than sin.   5(7)

❁◇❁

20th Yet it's truth that to any man may come the one extreme moment when he turns his back on his own nature and goes the contrary way.   9(9)

February

21st Now there was no time for anything but living, and exulting in living, and being glad and grateful, and perhaps, gradually and with unpractised pleasure, loving.   4(5:4)

22nd Knowing by rote is one thing. What the two equally innocent lovers experienced bore no resemblance to what they had thought they knew.   7(5)

23rd No use telling her that vocations strike from heaven like random arrows of God, by no means all because of unrequited love.   3(4)

February

24th 'The novice said he learned the song from his grandfather, who fought for the Cross at the taking of Jerusalem, and he found the tune so beautiful that it seemed to him holy. For the pilgrim who sang was not a monastic or a soldier, but a humble person who made the long journey out of love.'

'A proper and sanctified love,' pointed out Brother Cadfael, using words not entirely natural to him, for he thought of love as a self-sanctifying force, needing no apology. 3(1)

During chapter, a complaint was made about one of the young novices – he had been heard singing 'a secular song of scandalous import, purporting to be the lament of a Christian pilgrim imprisoned by the Saracens, and comforting himself by hugging to his breast the chemise given him at parting by his lover'.

✺

25th The young can be wildly generous, giving away their years and their youth for love, without thought of any gain.

11(3)

✺

26th The simplest and most temperate words are the best to express complex and intemperate feelings. 19(8)

February

27th Blessedness is what can be snatched out of the passing day, and put away to think of afterwards.

5(1)

✦❖✦

28th Where there's nothing at stake there's no barrier. Nothing to join, so nothing to divide.

19(8)

✦❖✦

29th Cadfael made his prayers. He had done what seemed best, he had had loyal and ingenious helpers, now he could only plump the whole matter confidingly into Saint Winifred's tolerant Welsh arms, remind her he was her distant kin, and leave the rest to her.

11(14)

March

March came in more lamb than lion, there were still windflowers in the woods, and the first primroses, unburned by frost, undashed and unmired by further rain, were just opening. 19(8)

March

1ˢᵗ Cadfael was about to urge her to let well alone and trust heaven to do justice, but then he had a sudden vision of heaven's justice as the Church sometimes applied it, in good but dreadful faith, with all the virtuous narrowness and pitilessness of minds blind and deaf to the infinite variety of humankind, its failings, and aspirations, and needs, and forgetful of all the Gospel reminders concerning publicans and sinners. And he thought of songbirds caged, drooping without air to play on the cords of their throats, without heart to sing, and knew that they might very well die. Half humanity was here in this lean dark girl beside him, and that half of humanity had its right to reason, determine and meddle, no less than the male half. After all, they were equally responsible for humankind continuing. There was not an archbishop or an abbot in the world who had not had a flesh and blood mother, and come of a passionate coupling. She would do as she thought fit, and so would he. 'Let all things be,' said Cadfael with a sigh. 'Who knows how much clearer the skies will be by tomorrow?'
19(ɪɪ)

Cadfael suspected that Daalny – a slave girl with a beautiful singing voice – was intending to free Tutilo, the 'Holy Thief', locked in the cell of Shrewsbury Abbey. Indeed, she did free him – and they both fled south-westward towards the borders of Wales.

March

2ⁿᵈ 'We Welsh recognise degrees,' said Cadfael. 'Theft, theft absolute, without excuse, is our most mortal offence, and therefore we hedge it about with degrees, things which are not theft absolute — taking openly by force, taking in ignorance, taking without leave, providing the offender owns to it, and taking to stay alive, where a beggar has starved three days — no man hangs in Wales for these. Even in dying, even in killing, we acknowledge degrees. We make a distinction between homicide and murder, and even the worst may sometimes be compounded for a lesser price than hanging.'

9(14)

3ʳᵈ All Welsh are kin, even if they slit one another's throats now and then, and manure their sparse and stony fields with fratricidal dead in tribal wars.

7(13)

March

4th Where there is no certainty the mind must turn to the light and not the shadow. 17(14)

✤

5th 'I have no skill at all with women, they confuse me utterly. I marvel how you have learned to deal with them so ably, you, a cloistered brother.'

'Both men and women partake of the same human nature. We both bleed when we're wounded. For every poor, silly woman, we can show plenty of poor, silly men. There are women as strong as any of us, and as able.' 1(9)

✤

6th Now and then the simplest explanation turns out to be the true one. 8(9)

March

7th Another's grief is not to be tolerated, if there can be anything
done to alleviate it.   10(4)

❖

8th Cadfael was not of the opinion that a man's main
business in this world was to save his own soul. There are other
ailing souls, as there are ailing bodies, in need of a hoist towards
health.   15(3)

❖

9th The more hotly you hasten, the more will you fall behind.
Remember that, and curb your impetuosity.   8(2)

March

10th 'It may be, Father Abbot,' the sub-prior said, 'that in this matter the Church will need to examine itself closely, for if it fails to contend against the evildoers wherever they may be found, its authority may fall into disrepute. Surely the battle against evil, within or without our pale, is as noble as a Crusade as the contention within the Holy Land. It is not to our credit if we stand by and let the evildoer go free. This man has deserted his brotherhood and abandoned his vows. He must be brought back to answer for it.'

'If you esteem him as a creature so fallen from grace,' said the abbot coldly, 'you should observe what the Rule has to say of such a case, in the twenty-eighth chapter, where it is written: "Drive out the wicked man from among you." '

'But we have not driven him out. He has not waited the judgement nor answered for his offences, but taken himself off secretly in the night to our discomfiture.'

'Even so,' murmured Cadfael as to himself but very audibly, unable to resist the temptation, 'in the same chapter the Rule commands us: "If the faithless brother leaves you, *let him go*." '   19(13)

Before the Church was able to dispense its own punishment on the 'Holy Thief',
for attempting to steal the supposed relics of St Winifred, Brother Tutilo
escaped from the abbey cell at Shrewsbury and fled the region.

March

11th If two hold fast together they stand steadily, but if one holds aloof the other may find his feet betraying him in slippery places. Better a limping prop than a solid rock for ever out of reach of the stretched hand.

12(9)

12th Great age is no blessing, when the body's strength outlives the mind.

9(4)

13th He prayed as he breathed, forming no words and making no specific requests, only holding in his heart, like broken birds in cupped hands, all those people who were in stress of grief.

1(7)

March

14th Heaven has need of a little time. Even miracles have their times. Half our lives in this world are spent waiting. It is needful to wait with faith. 10(11)

15th God disposes all. From the highest to the lowest extreme of a man's scope, whatever justice and retribution can reach him, so can grace. 2(12)

16th We must see every man clearly, with his words and his deeds upon him, and not hasten to cover him from sight with this universal cloak of heresy. Once the word is spoken, the man himself may become invisible. And therefore expendable! 16(5)

March

17th I loved him from before I knew what love was. All I knew was how much it hurt, that I could not endure to be away from him, that I followed and would be with him, and he would not see me, would not speak with me, put me roughly from his side as often as I clung. I was already promised to another, who was more than half his world. I was too young then to know that the measure of his rejection of me was the measure of how much he wanted me. But when I came to understand what it was that tortured me, then I knew that he went daily in the selfsame pain.   9(12)

Despite being betrothed from a child to Elis ap Cynan, Cristina secretly loved his foster-brother and cousin, Eluid ap Griffith. Eluid, in turn, loved Cristina, but denied his feelings so as not to hurt Elis. It was only after Elis fell in love with another that Cristina and Eluid revealed their true long-held feelings for each other.

18th Girl children are always years older than their brothers at the same age in years, and see more accurately and jealously.   9(12)

March

19th An agreement to put off contention to a more convenient time is better than no agreement at all, and the need to look over a shoulder every hour or so.   16(1)

❋✦❋

20th She had always thought of the Welsh with fear and distrust, as uncouth savages; and suddenly here was this trim and personable young man whose eyes dazzled and whose cheeks flamed at meeting her gaze. She thought of him much.   9(2)

Spring

A time for all manner of births and beginnings, and for putting death out of mind.   9(15)

❖❖❖

21st Love is the one thing with which you must never dispense. Without it, what use are you to us or to any? Granted there are ways and ways of loving, yet for all there is a warmth needed, and if that fire goes out it cannot be rekindled.   9(8)

❖❖❖

22nd I think you loved him as much as he would let you. As he could let you. Some men have not the gift.   4(2:1)

March

23rd

Love and hate are often bed-fellows. You need not question either.

7(10)

❦❖❦

24th

If there's a hair shirt anywhere within reach he will claim it and wear it. A lifelong penitent, that lad, God knows for what imagined sins, for I never knew him so much as break a rule since he entered as a novice, and seeing he was no more than eighteen when he took his first vows, I doubt if he'd had time to do the world much harm up to then. But there are some born to do penance by nature. Maybe they lift the load for some of us who take it quite comfortably that we're humankind, and not angels. If the overflow from his penitence and piety washes off a few of my shortcomings, may it redound to him for credit in the accounting. And I shan't complain.

15(1)

Believing, wrongly, that he had committed a terrible sin in his youth, Brother Haluin endured years of remorse and self-punishment.

March

25th 'As if only his body is here, and his spirit gone elsewhere until the house is again furbished and clean and waiting to be lived in.'

A sound biblical analogy, Cadfael considered, for certainly he had himself cast out the devils that inhabited him, and the dwelling they vacated might well lie empty for a while, all the more if there was to be that unlooked-for and improbable act of healing, after all. For however this prolonged withdrawal might resemble dying, he would not die. Then we had better keep a good watch, thought Cadfael, taking the parable to its fitting close, and make sure seven devils worse than the first never manage to get a foot in the door while he's absent.

15(2)

While working on the roof of one of the abbey buildings, Brother Haluin slipped and fell, seriously injuring himself. Although not expected to live, he regained consciousness and made a miraculous recovery. The fall, however, left him a permanent cripple.

March

26th 'We live in a contentious world,' said Cadfael, who had lived more than half his life in the thick of the battles. 'Who says peace would be good for us?' 4(1:1)

27th The ugliness that man can do to man might cast a shadow between you and the certainty of the justice and mercy God can do to him hereafter. It takes half a lifetime to reach the spot where eternity is always visible, and crude injustice of the hour shrivels out of sight. You'll come to it when the time's right. 2(3)

28th Under the certainty of Heaven, nothing is ever quite certain. 7(11)

March

29th Nothing so wonderful had been heard in the choir of the church. This was an ageless voice that might have belonged to a child or an angel. Blessed be the human condition, thought Cadfael, which allows us marred and fallible creatures who are neither angels nor children to make sounds like these, that belong in another world. Unlooked-for mercies, undeserved grace! 19(11)

※◈※

30th God's plans for us, however infallibly good, may not take the form that we expect and demand. 2(12)

※◈※

31st Never go looking for disaster. Expect the best, and walk discreetly as to invite it, and then leave all to God. 6(8)

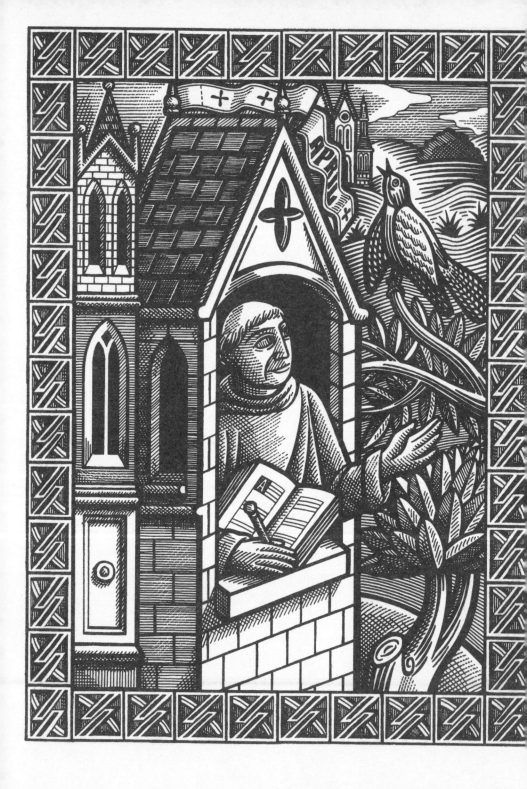

April

The birds were nesting, and the meadow flowers just beginning to thrust their buds up through the new grass, and the sun to rise a little higher in the sky every noon. 18(1)

April

1st Brother Cadfael approached April in a mood of slightly restless hopefulness. True, there were troubles in the world, as there always had been. The vexed affairs of England, torn in two by two cousins contending for the throne, had still no visible hope of a solution. But for some months now there had been very little fighting between them, whether from exhaustion or policy, and a strange calm had settled over the country, almost peace. All in all, there was room for some cautious optimism, and the very freshness and lustre of the Spring forbade despondency, even had despondency been among Cadfael's propensities.   18(1)

2nd Miracles have nothing to do with reason. Miracles contradict reason, overturn reason, make game of reason, they strike clean across mere human deserts, and deliver and save where they will. If they made sense they would not be miracles.   1(11)

3rd Portents can arise, miracles can be delivered, either from angels or devils.   1(3)

April

4th To live misused, ill-fed, without respite from labour, was still life, with a sky above it, and trees and flowers and birds around it, colour and season and beauty. Life, even so lived, was a friend. Death was a stranger.

4(4:4)

5th Death falls upon children who never did harm to any, upon old men, who in their lives have done good to many, and yet are brutally and senselessly slain. Never let it shake your faith that there is a balance hereafter. What you see is only a broken piece from a perfect whole.

4(4:4)

6th Love, of itself, is not sin, cannot be sin, though it may lead to sin.

13(2)

April

7th Just for a moment she rained tears like the spring thaw, and then she glinted radiance like the spring sun. There was so much to grieve over, and so much to celebrate, she did not know which to do first, and essayed both together, like April. But her age was April, and the hopeful sunshine won.   2(2)

Having escaped from Shrewsbury Castle (besieged by King Stephen in 1138), Godith Adeney found refuge at the abbey, disguised as a boy. Although many supporters of the Empress Maud were killed in the fighting, or hung from the castle walls, Cadfael brought some good news — her father was neither dead, nor wounded, nor captured, but had evaded the clutches of Stephen's men and was on his way to Normandy.

8th Where the sun shines, there whoever's felt the cold will gather.   10(1)

9th Don't reach for the halo too soon. You have plenty of time to enjoy yourself, even a little maliciously sometimes, before you settle down to being a saint.   3(11)

April

10th The Benedictines had very little hold in Wales, Welshmen preferred their own ancient Celtic Christianity, the solitary hermitage of the self-exiled saint and the homely little college of Celtic monks rather than the shrewd and vigorous foundations that looked to Rome. 3(8)

11th Even the very system of bishoprics galled the devout adherents of the old, saintly Celtic church, that had no worldly trappings, courted no thrones, but rather withdrew from the world into the blessed solitude of thought and prayer. 1(3)

12th No one need be an angel to sing like one. 19(8)

April

13th The want of Welsh was a frustration no longer so easy to bear. She brought his dinner, and sat by him while he ate, and the same want of words troubled her. It was all very well teaching him simple words and phrases in Welsh by touching the thing she meant, but how to set about pouring out to him, as she would have liked, all that was happening? The helplessness of talking at all made their meetings almost silent, but sometimes they did speak aloud, he in English, she in Welsh, saying things because they could not be contained, things that would be understood by the other only in some future day, though the tone might convey at least the sense of friendship, like a kind of restrained caress. Thus they conducted two little monologues which yet were an exchange and a comfort. Sometimes, though they did not know it, they were even answering each other's questions.

1(7)

*In 1137, while professing doubts about his vocation, Brother John went
to Wales with Prior Robert's party. He met the Welsh girl, Annest, and they
fell in love — neither, however, could speak the other's language.*

April

14th Love makes men do terrible things, even to their friends.

1(8)

❀❖❀

15th Blameless young women have before now been taken in by black-hearted villains, even murderers; and black-hearted villains and murderers have been deeply devoted to blameless young women, contradicting their own nature in this one perverse tenderness.

2(6)

❀❖❀

16th There is nothing evil there. Neither earth nor water nor air have any part in man's ill-doing.

6(6)

April

17th 'Money!' said the Welshman in the most extraordinary of tones, at once curious, derisory and revolted. He knew about money, of course, and even understood its use, but as an aberration in human relations. In the rural parts of Wales, which indeed were almost all of Wales, it was hardly used at all, and hardly needed. Provision was made in the code for all necessary exchange of goods and services, nobody was so poor as to be without the means of living, and beggars were unknown. The kinship took care of its helpless members, and every house was open as of right. The minted coins that had seeped in through the marches were a pointless eccentricity.

1(3)

The 'code', or the Laws of Hywel Dda, *governed Wales until the middle of the sixteenth century, when it was superseded by English law. Hywel Dda, the ninth-century king of Wales, is widely credited with compiling the first Welsh law code (even if, in reality, he may only have been responsible for the unification and orderly arrangement of pre-existing law).*

18th Money brings men together. 4(1:2)

19th Have you never hunted zealously in all the wrong places for something you desired not to find? 1(6)

April

20th He had it all planned beforehand. That was all a show, all that wonder and amazement, and asking who Saint Winifred was, and where to find her. He knew it all along. He'd already picked her out from those he'd discovered neglected in Wales, and decided she was the one most likely to be available, as well as the one to shed most lustre on him. But it had to come out into the open by miraculous means. There'll be another prodigy whenever he needs his way smoothed for him, until he gets the saint's relics here safely installed in the church, to his glory. It's a great enterprise, he means to climb high on the strength of it. So he starts out with a vision, and a prodigious healing, and divine grace leading his footsteps. It's plain as the nose on your face.   I(I)

In 1137, Robert Pennant, prior of Shrewsbury Abbey, led a party of monks into Wales to obtain the sacred relics of St Winifred. He later wrote a Life of the saint, which ended with an account of the journey and the triumphant installation of the saint's remains in the abbey church. Robert became abbot of Shrewsbury in about 1148.

21st If I have guessed right, there is here a problem beyond my wit or yours to solve. I promise my endeavour. The ending is not mine, it belongs only to God. But what I can do, I will do.   II(10)

April

22^{**nd**} 'But both prince and bishop have given us their blessing, and commended our cause to you. Moreover, we have heard, and they have agreed, that the saint in her stay here among you has been much neglected, and may well wish to be received where greater honour will be paid to her.'

'In my church,' said the Welsh priest humbly, 'I have never heard that the saints desired honour for themselves, but rather to honour God rightly. So I do not presume to know what the saint's will may be in this matter. That you and your house should desire to honour *her* rightly, that is another matter, and very proper. But . . . This blessed virgin lived out her miraculously restored life in this place, and no other. Here she died for the second time, and here is buried, and even if my people have neglected her, being human and faulty, yet they always knew that she was here among them, and at a pinch they could rely on her, and for a Welsh saint I think that counts for much.'

1(2)

Despite having obtained official permission to dig up St Winifred's bones and take them back to England, Prior Robert found that the Welsh villagers of Gwytherin (where she was buried) were hostile to the idea — even though they themselves had neglected to maintain the saint's grave.

April

23rd Saint Winifred was here. She had lived many years as an abbess after her brief martyrdom and miraculous restoration, yet he thought of her as that devout, green girl, in romantic love with celibacy and holiness, who had fled from Prince Cradoc's advances as from the devil himself. By some perverse severance of the heart in two he could feel both for her and for the desperate lover, so roughly molten out of the flesh and presumably exterminated in the spirit. Did anyone ever pray for him? He was in greater need than Winifred. In the end, perhaps the only prayers he ever benefited by were Winifred's prayers. She was Welsh, and capable of detachment and subtlety. She might well have put in a word for him, to reassemble his liquefied person and congeal it again into the shape of a man. A chastened man, doubtless, but still the same shape as before. Even a saint may take pleasure, in retrospect, in having been once desired.

1(8)

According to medieval legend, St Winifred lived at Holywell in the seventh century. Prince Cradoc tried to seduce her, but when she fled, he chased after her and cut off her head with his sword. Winifred's uncle, St Beuno, miraculously restored her to life. Cradoc, however, suffered a most dreadful fate — his flesh turned to liquid and vanished entirely into the ground: 'as to the body expunged out of the world, as to the soul, the fearful imagination dared not guess'.

24th You'll never get to be a saint if you deny the bit of the devil in you.

3(11)

57

April

25th Unrequited love. It's no new problem. The lightning strikes where it will. One flames, and the other remains cold. Distance is the only cure.

4(2:2)

26th At this moment there was no resistance he could offer, and no repayment he could make, but to bow his head fervently among the rest and give profound thanks for present mercies.

5(4)

27th Even the pursuit of perfection may be sin, if it infringes the rights and needs of another soul. Better to fail a little, by turning aside to lift up another, than to pass by him in haste to reach our own reward, and leave him to solitude and despair. Better to labour in lameness, in fallibility, but holding up others who falter, than to stride forward alone.

12(11)

April

28th There are true things I will not tell you, and questions I will not answer, but everything I do tell you, and every answer I give you, shall be the truth. 13(12)

✦

29th It is a terrible responsibility, thought Cadfael, who had never aspired to ordination, to have the grace of God committed to a man's hands, to be privileged and burdened to play a part in other people's lives, to promise them salvation in baptism, to lock their lives together in matrimony, to hold the key to purgatory at their departing. If I have meddled, he thought devoutly, and God knows I have, when need was and there was no better man to attempt it, at least I have meddled only as a fellow-sinner, tramping the same road, not as a *vicomte* of heaven, stooping to raise up. 15(8)

✦

30th 'We deal with what is,' said Cadfael. 'Leave what might have been to eyes that can see it plain.' 2(12)

May

On a fine bright morning in early May Brother Cadfael was up long before Prime, pricking out cabbage seedlings, and his thoughts were all on birth, growth and fertility.

1(1)

May

1^{**st**} 'I know my herbs,' said Cadfael. 'They have fixed properties, and follow sacred rules. Human creatures do not so. And I cannot even wish they did. I would not have one scruple of their complexity done away, it would be lamentable loss.' 4(3:1)

2^{**nd**} There are plants some people cannot handle without coming to grief. No one knows the reason. We learn by observing.

13(1)

3^{**rd**} Every man has within him only one life and one nature to give to the service of God, and if there was but one way of doing that, celibate within the cloister, procreation and birth would cease, the world would be depeopled, and neither within nor without the Church would God receive worship. 17(4)

May

4th It is well that a man should know his own work. 3(2)

***

5th Cadfael went to his bed, and slept as soon as he lay down. He had the gift. There was no profit in lying awake fretting for what would, in any case, have to be faced on awakening, and he had long ago sloughed off the unprofitable. It took too much out of a man, of what would be needed hereafter. 6(5)

***

6th The only reason I know myself is because I *am* myself.

4(4:1)

May

7th Cleverness and wisdom are not inevitable yoke-fellows.   5(2)

※❖※

8th He saw no reason why he should expect to be singled out
for healing, but he said that he offered his pain freely, who had
nothing else to give. Not to buy grace, but of his goodwill to give and
want nothing in return. And further, it seems that thus having accepted his pain out of love, his pain left him.   10(11)

※❖※

9th Brother Cadfael saw all things in cautious balance.   4(3:2)

May

10th 'We shall have to call up the priest and your prior, and tell them exactly what's happened. What else can we do? I'm sorry to have killed the fellow, I never meant to, but I can't say I feel any *guilt* about it.'

Nor did he expect any blame. The truth was always the best way. Cadfael felt a reluctant affection for such innocence. The world was going to damage it sooner or later, but one undeserved accusation had so far failed even to bruise it, he still trusted men to be reasonable.

1(10)

Engelard, a landless Saxon youth, tried to stop a murderer from escaping, and accidentally broke the man's neck and killed him. But, because the man was a monk, whose crime involved Church affairs, Engelard's confession was likely to cause a fearful scandal to break 'to smirch the abbey of Shrewsbury, and all the forces of the Benedictine order'. Cadfael reasoned, therefore, that the authorities would avoid bringing disrepute on the Church by blaming Engelard for both killings — murderer and murderer's victim.

11th Beware of inverted pride! Moderation in all things is not the most spectacular path to perfection, but it is the safest and the most modest.

13(2)

May

12th 'Brother, a great wonder! There came a traveller here in great pain from a malignant illness, and made such outcry that all of us in the hostel were robbed of sleep. And the prior took a few of the petals we saved from the chapel, and floated them in holy water, and gave them to this poor soul to drink, and afterwards we carried him out into the yard and let him kiss the foot of Saint Winifred's reliquary. And instantly he was eased of his pain, and before we laid him in his bed again he was asleep. He feels nothing, he slumbers like a child! Oh, brother, we are the means of astonishing grace!'

'Ought it to astonish you so much?' demanded Brother Cadfael censoriously, for he was considerably more taken aback than he would admit. 'If you had any faith in what we have brought from Wales, you should not be amazed that it accomplishes wonders along the way.' But by the same token, he thought honestly, I should!   I(II)

Cadfael was surprised to discover that St Winifred was accomplishing miracles far from the place where her body lay. Prior Robert and all the brothers of Shrewsbury Abbey believed that the wooden reliquary held the Welsh saint's remains. Brother Cadfael knew otherwise. It held the corpse of Brother Columbanus, which he had secretly sealed inside.

May

13th Universal grace, whether it manifested itself in Wales, or England, or the Holy Land, or wheresoever, was to be hailed with universal gratitude.

1(12)

14th It is a blessed thing, on the whole, to live in slightly dull times. But there was still a morsel somewhere in Cadfael that itched if the hush continued too long. A little excitement, after all, need not be mischief, and does sound a pleasant counterpoint to the constant order, however much that may be loved and however faithfully served.

18(1)

15th He poured out fervent thanks, and promises he might never be able to keep, though he meant them with all his heart.

7(14)

May

16th He was a child of the cloister, not long a full brother, and entrusted with his particular charge by reason of his undoubted deserving, tempered by the reserve that was felt about admitting child oblates to full office, at least until they had been mature for a number of years. An unreasonable reserve, Cadfael had always felt, seeing that the child oblates were regarded as the perfect innocents, equivalent to the angels, while the *conversi*, those who came voluntarily and in maturity to the monastic life, were the fighting saints, those who had endured and mastered their imperfections. So Saint Anselm had classified them, and ordered them never to attempt reciprocal reproaches, never to feel envy. But still the *conversi* were preferred for the responsible offices, perhaps as having experience of the deceits and complexities and temptations of the world around them. But the care of an altar, its light, its draperies, the special prayers belonging to it, this could well be the charge of an innocent.

13(1)

May

17th No more oblates, the abbot was reflecting ruefully, and thanking God for it. No more taking these babes out of their cradles and severing them from the very sight and sound of women, half the creation stolen out of their world. How can they be expected to deal capably at last with something as strange and daunting to them as dragons? Sooner or later a woman must cross their path, terrible as an army with banners, and these wretched children without arms or armour to withstand the onslaught! We wrong women, and we wrong these boys, to send them unprepared into maturity, whole men, defenceless against the first pricking of the flesh. In defending them from perils we have deprived them of the means to defend themselves. Well, no more now! Those who enter here henceforward will be of manhood's years, enter of their own will, bear their own burdens. 13(2)

In his late teens, Brother Eluric, an oblate (having entered the monastery at three years of age), was charged with delivering the annual rose rent to the widow, Judith Perle. He found himself haunted with uninvited feelings of love towards the woman and, racked with remorse for imagined sins, begged the abbot to release him from the painful duty.

May

18th There were drawbacks in any course of life. Neither inside nor outside the cloister could a man have everything.   5(10)

19th 'No one should take to the cloistered life as a second-best. It must be embraced out of genuine desire, or not at all. It is not enough to wish to escape from the world without, you must be on fire for the world within.'

'Was it so with you?'

Cadfael considered that in silence for a brief, cautious while. 'I came late to it, and it may be that my fire burned somewhat dully,' he said honestly at length, 'but it gave light enough to show me the road to what I wanted. I was running towards, not away.'   13(1)

20th Truth is never a wrong answer.   6(14)

May

21st As every brother within here knows, there's no questioning a vocation. It comes when it will, and there's no refusal.

15(1)

※❖※

22nd The brothers doggedly pursued their chosen regime, service after service, chapter and Mass and the hours of work, because life could only be sustained by refusing to let it be disrupted, by war, catastrophe or death.

2(2)

※❖※

23rd Those who have been blinded by too great a light do not see, cannot afford to see, the pain they cause.

8(1)

May

24th 'As a brother of the Order,' said Cadfael, 'I would wish to keep my hands from violence against any, but for all that, I hope I would not turn my back if I saw innocence or helplessness being abused. Bear in mind even the bishops carry a crook, meant to protect the flock as well as guide it.' 11(1)

25th Cadfael would not go gladly, turning his back upon a murder unavenged, justice out of kilter, a wrong that might never be set right. 15(10)

26th You are your own master, however ill you master yourself. 8(6)

May

27th 'The longer I study here, the more I begin to think well of heretics. Perhaps I am one, after all. When they all professed to believe in God, and tried to live in a way pleasing to him, how could they hate one another so much?'

The precentor had turned a page of Origen and replied tranquilly: 'It all comes of trying to formulate what is too vast and mysterious to be formulated. You may have lost your saving innocence, but if you are sinking, it's in a morass of other men's words, not your own. They never hold so fast. You have only to close the book.'

16(10)

In 1136, Elave, the 'Heretic's Apprentice', went on a pilgrimage to the Holy Land with his master, William of Lythwood. On his return, he was accused of heresy and brought before the Church authorities to face the charge. While waiting to argue his case, Elave studied several books, including the writings of Origen — the third-century Greek Father of the Church, whose teachings were also considered heretical.

28th 'Well, well!' said Cadfael silently to himself, and left the insoluble to the solver of all problems. 1(4)

May

29th 'We never intended evil, but we committed a terrible sacrilege. Here in the church, behind one of the holy altars – we couldn't bear it . . . We lay together as lovers do!'

'You love this girl?' asked Cadfael after some thought, and very placidly.

'Yes, I *do* love her! With all my heart I want her for my wife.'

'I think,' said Cadfael, 'where mutual love is, I find it hard to consider any place too holy to house it. Our Lady, according to the miracles they tell of her, has been known to protect even the guilty who sinned out of love. You might try a few prayers to her, that will do no harm. Don't trouble too much for what was done under such strong compulsion and pure of any evil intent.'

7(7)

Whilst hiding in a dark recess behind one of the church altars in
Shrewsbury Abbey, Lilliwin, the 'Sanctuary Sparrow', made love to Rannilt,
a poor servant-girl. Both were inexperienced in love and, when they
realised what they'd done, both quaked in terror of damnation.

May

30th Know well the sacredness of sanctuary. It is not shelter against sin, it is the provision of a time of calm, when the guilty may examine his soul, and the innocent confide in his salvation. But it may not be violated. It has a period, but until that time is spent it is holy. 7(2)

Pursued by an angry mob of townsmen, Lilliwin took refuge in the church of Shrewsbury Abbey and was granted forty days' sanctuary by the abbot.

31st Brother Cadfael wondered if prayer can have a retro-spective effect upon events, as well as influencing the future. What had happened had already happened, yet would he have found the same situation if he had not gone straight into the church with the passionate urge to commit to prayer the direction of his own efforts, which seemed to him so barren? It was a most delicate and complex theological problem, never, as far as he knew, raised before, or if raised, no theologian had ventured to write on the subject, prob-ably for fear of being accused of heresy. 4(4:3)

June

The sun came out over the earth like a warm hand stroking, the seeds stirred in the ground and put forth green blades, and a foam of flowers burst forth over garden and meadow.

13(1)

June

1ˢᵗ It was a matter of principle, or perhaps of honour, with Brother Cadfael, when a door opened before him suddenly and unexpectedly, to accept the offer and walk through it. 18(1)

※◇※

2ⁿᵈ 'Bear in mind,' said the nun, 'that our doors are not closed against any woman in need, and the quiet is not reserved for those who have taken vows. The time may come when you truly need a place to be apart, time for thought and rest, even time to recover lost courage. Wait, bear with things as they are. But if ever you need a place to hide, for a little while or a long while, come to the monastery and bring all your frets in with you, and you shall find a refuge for as long as you need, with no vows taken, never unless you come to it with a whole heart. And I will keep the door against the world until you see fit to go forth again.' 13(3)

※◇※

3ʳᵈ Draw off, and try something else, but never give up. 5(8)

June

4th 'Strange! When he went out, he did not seem to me evil, or malicious, or aware of guilt. Only bewildered! As though he found himself where he had never thought or meant to be, in some place he could not even recognise, and not knowing how he made his way there.'

'In some sort,' said Cadfael soberly, 'I think that is truth. He was like a man who has taken the first slippery step into a marsh, and then cannot draw back, and at every step forward sinks the deeper. From one sin to another, he went where he was driven. No wonder if the place where he arrived was utterly alien to him, and the face that waited for him in a mirror there was one he did not even know, a terrible stranger.'

13(14)

5th Without faith nothing is accomplished.

7(4)

June

6th When men have elected a villain, and one from comfortably outside their own ranks, without roots or kin they need feel nothing for him, he is hardly a man, has no blood to be shed or heart to be broken, and whatever else needs a scapegoat will be laid on him heartily and in the conviction of righteousness. Nor will reason have much say in the matter. 7(7)

7th He hung over the shivering stranger, between fascinated horror at viewing a murderer close, and surprised pity at seeing so miserable a human being, where a brutal monster should have been. 7(1)

8th To overcome the lures of evil is all that can be required of mortals. 17(14)

June

9th Brothers and lay brothers served at the leper-hospital at their own request. It was not unknown that attendant should become attended, but there was never want of another volunteer to replace and nurse him.   5(1)

✦

10th The monk had no fear of contagion, since he never gave a thought to the peril, all his energy being absorbed into the need. Nor would he ever be surprised, or complain, if at last contagion did seize upon him and draw him even closer to the people he served.   5(1)

✦

11th He had dressed more and viler sores than he troubled to remember, and discovered live hearts and vigorous minds within the mottled shells he tended.   5(1)

June

12th He had bought her, but there was enough of cold sense in him, below his doting, to know that he had to buy her over and over again if he wanted to keep her.   7(4)

13th Leave agonising too much over your sins, black as they are, there isn't a confessor in the land who hasn't heard worse and never turned a hair. It's a kind of arrogance to be so certain you're past redemption.   1(9)

14th You need to use what you know and make use of what you can do.   5(8)

June

15th 'It's true,' said Cadfael, 'now and again my feet itch for the
road. But when it comes down to it, as roads go, the road
home is as good as any.' 18(14)

16th His body is recovering well. And as for the part of his
mind that's astray, my being here won't cure it. It will come
back of itself one day, or it will cease to be missed. 6(5)

17th Miracles may be simply divine manipulation of ordinary
circumstances. 19(10)

June

18th If there must be fighting, if there must be deaths, let it happen as God wills, not as ambitious and evil men contrive. Those lives we cannot save, at least let us not help to destroy.

4(5:6)

19th The application of Cadfael's herbal remedies soothed and placated the mind as well as the skin.

5(1)

20th God is still looking your way.

3(7)

Summer

T he summer season was at its height, and promising rich harvest, for the spring had been mild and moist after plenteous early snows, and June and July hot and sunny. 4(1:1)

21st (The Eve of St Winifred's Translation)

'Trouble your head no more,' said Cadfael, 'but think only of the morrow, when you approach Saint Winifred. Both she and God see you all, and have no need to be told what your needs are. All you have to do is wait in quiet for whatever will be. For whatever it may be, it will not be wanton: Say your prayers, think quietly what you should do, do it, and sleep. There is no man living, neither king nor emperor, can do more or better, or trust in a better harvest.' 10(6)

Cadfael was talking to Rhun, an orphan, who had travelled to Shrewsbury from his aunt's home in the Cotswolds to celebrate St Winifred's festival. Despite having a crippled right leg, Rhun walked the whole way on foot, supported by crutches. It took him three weeks.

22nd (St Winifred's Translation)

Something wonderful happened. When they turned their heads to look at each other, they saw only mated eyes and a halo of sunshine. They did not speak at all. They had no need of speech. 10(9)

June

23ʳᵈ For the very intensity of all that mortal emotion gathered thus between confining walls and beneath one roof, it was impossible to withdraw the eyes for an instant from the act of worship on which it was centred, or the mind from the words of the office. There had been times, in the past, when Cadfael's thoughts had strayed during Mass to worrying at other problems, and working out other intents. It was not so now. Throughout, he was unaware of a single face in all that throng, only of the presence of humankind, in whom his own identity was lost; or, perhaps, into whom his own identity expanded like air, to fill every part of the whole.   10(9)

24ᵗʰ It was a lot to ask, but miracles do sometimes happen.

19(12)

25ᵗʰ Take heart, nothing is ever quite what it seems.   6(14)

June

26th A great, shuddering sigh went round nave, choir, transepts and all, wherever there were human creatures watching and listening. And after the sigh the quivering murmur of a gathering storm, whether of tears or laughter there was no telling, but the air shook with its passion. And then the outcry, the loosing of both tears and laughter, in a gale of wonder and praise. From stone walls and lofty, arched roof, from rood-loft and transept arcades, the echoes flew and rebounded, and the candles that had stood so still and tall shook and guttered in the gale. All took up the chant. A miracle, a miracle, a miracle . . . And in the midst he stood erect and still, even a little bewildered, braced sturdily on his two long, shapely legs.

10(9)

In 1141, the young boy Rhun approached St Winifred's altar in the abbey church and, as he did so, his crippled leg was miraculously straightened.

June

27th Where the seed lights, the herb grows. And there's nothing like hard usage and drought to drive its roots deep.

16(6)

✦

28th It is not enough to abstain from evil, there must also be an outgoing goodness. The company of the blessed may extend justifiably to embrace even men who have been great sinners, yet also great lovers of their fellow men, such as have never turned away their eyes from other men's needs, but have done them such good as they might, and as little harm as they must. 12(11)

✦

29th In this glowing evening light Cadfael looked upon the world, from the roses in the garden to the wrought stones of the cloister walls, and found it unquestionably beautiful. 16(2)

June

30th It was as if a part of him, heart, mind, soul, whatever that essence might be, had not so much retired as come home to take seisin of a heritage here, his from his birth. And yet Cadfael remembered and acknowledged with gratitude and joy the years of his sojourning in the world, the lusty childhood and venturous youth, the taking of the Cross and the passion of the Crusade, the women he had known and loved, the years of his seafaring off the coast of the Holy Kingdom of Jerusalem, all that pilgrimage that had led him here at last to his chosen retreat. None of it wasted, however foolish and amiss, nothing lost, nothing vain, all of it somehow fitting him to the narrow niche where now he served and rested. God had given him a sign, he had no need to regret anything, only to lay all open and own it his. For God's viewing, not for man's.   10(2)

July

✣❖✣

In the herb-garden, shaded along one side by its high hedge from the declining sun, the heavy fragrances of the day hung like a spell.

4(1:1)

July

1st Aim at making everybody happy, and if that's within reach, why stir up any kind of unpleasantness? 1(10)

2nd There has many a man gone through that gate without a safe-conduct, who will reach heaven ahead of some who were escorted through with absolution and ceremony, and had their affairs in order. Some who claim they have done great good may have to give place to poor wretches who have done wrong and acknowledge it, and have tried to make amends. 4(4:4)

3rd I have never held that rank or trade is valued before God. 16(2)

July

4th It is not for them to question or reason with inadequate minds, but to accept with unquestioning faith. Truth is set before them, they have only to believe. It is the perverse and perilous who have the arrogance to bring mere fallible reason to bear on what is ineffable.

16(2)

5th The failure of the priesthood to set an example of piety and simplicity helps to turn people to false prophets and dissenting sects. The Church has a duty also to purge its own shortcomings.

16(2)

6th 'It's a grave matter to disagree with the Church,' said the layman. 'It's not for us to know better than the priests, not where faith's concerned. Listen and say Amen, that's my advice.'

16(4)

July

7th 'He said that if the Father and the Son were of one and the same substance, as the creed calls them consubstantial, then the entry of the Son into humankind must mean also the entry of the Father, taking to himself and making divine that which he had united with the godhead. And therefore the Father and the Son alike knew the suffering and the death and the resurrection, and as one partake in our redemption.'

'It is the Patripassian heresy! Sabellius was excommunicated for it, and for his other errors. Noetus of Smyrna preached it to his ruin. This is indeed a dangerous venture. He is digging a pit for his own soul.'

16(2)

The earliest form of the Patripassian heresy was taught by Noetus of Smyrna, who was excommunicated for preaching the doctrines at around the end of the second century AD. The teaching was brought to Rome by one of his disciples. There, in the third century, Sabellius preached a form of the doctrine known as Sabellianism. He too was eventually condemned as a heretic and excommunicated.

8th He said if the first was Father, and the second Son, how could they be co-eternal and co-equal? And as to the Spirit, he could not see how it could be equal with either Father or Son if it emanated from them. Moreover, he saw no need for a third, creation, salvation and all things being complete in Father and Son. Thus the third served only to satisfy the vision of those who think in threes, as the song-makers and soothsayers do, and all those who deal with enchantment.'

16(2)

July

9th 'There are things I want to know. How did Father and Son first become three? Who first wrote of them as three, to confuse us all? How can there be three, all equal, who are yet not three but one?'

'As the three lobes of the clover leaf are three and equal but united in one leaf,' suggested the precentor.

'And the four-leaved clover, that brings luck? What is the fourth, humankind? Or are we the stem of the threesome, that binds all together?'

The precentor shook his head over him, but with unperturbed serenity and a tolerant grin. 'Never write a book, son! You would certainly be made to burn it!'   16(10)

10th Sleep easy, for God is awake.   3(4)

11th Grace is not a river into which a man can dip his pail at will, but a fountain that plays when it lists, and when it lists is dry and still.   13(2)

July

12th I can't believe that babes are born into the world already rotten with sin. How can that be true? A creature new and helpless, barely into this world, how can it ever have done wrong? I say that it's only his own deeds, bad and good, that a man will have to answer for in the judgement, and that's what will save or damn him. Though it's not often I've known a man so bad as to make me believe in damnation. There was a father of the Church, once, as I heard tell, in Alexandria, who held that in the end everyone would find salvation. Even the fallen angels would return to their fealty, even the devil would repent and make his way back to God.   16(4)

The 'father of the Church' was Origen (or Oregenes Adamantius), who was born in about AD 185, probably in Alexandria. A great Christian writer and scholar, he became head of the Catechetical School in Alexandria. He died at Tyre — after surviving torture and imprisonment — in about 254.

13th Don't bury your talent. It is better to cut too deep a course than to stagnate and grow foul.   16(15)

14th Nobody does ill to keep faith.   3(7)

July

15th 'The Church tells us there's no salvation but by grace, not by works. A man can do nothing to save himself, being born sinful.'

'I don't believe that. Would the good God have made a creature so imperfect that he can have no free will of his own to choose between right and wrong? We can make our own way towards salvation, or down into the muck, and at the last we must every one stand by his own acts in the judgement. If we are men we ought to make our own way towards grace, not sit on our hams and wait for it to lift us up.'

'No, no, we're taught differently, Men are fallen by the first fall, and incline towards evil. They can never do good but by the grace of God.'

'And I say they *can* and do! A man *can* choose to avoid sin and do justly, of his own will, and his own will is the gift of God, and meant to be used. Why should a man get credit for leaving it all to God? We think about what we're doing daily with our hands, to earn a living. What fools we should be not to give a thought to what we're doing with our souls, to earn an eternal life. *Earn* it,' he said with emphasis, 'not wait to be given it unearned.'   16(4)

July

16th I do believe we have been given free will, and can and must use it to choose between right and wrong, if we are men and not beasts. Surely it is the least of what we owe, to try and make our way towards salvation by right action. I never denied divine grace. Surely it is the greatest grace that we are given this power to choose, and the strength to make right use of it. And see, if there is a last judgement, it will not and cannot be of God's grace, but of what every man has done with it, whether he buried his talent or turned it to good profit. It is for our own actions we shall answer, when the day comes. 16(15)

17th A Seljuk Turk or a Saracen can cut down Christians in battle or throw stray pilgrims into dungeons, and still be tolerated and respected, even if he's held to be already damned. But if a Christian steps a little aside in his beliefs he becomes anathema. Cadfael had seen it years ago in the east, in the admittedly beleaguered Christian churches. Hard pressed by enemies, it was on their own they turned most savagely. 16(2)

18th What are wits for, unless a man uses them? 16(5)

July

19ᵗʰ The readings during the meal had been from the writings of Saint Augustine, of whom Cadfael was not as fond as he might have been. There is a certain unbending rigidity about Augustine that offers little compassion to anyone with whom he disagrees. Cadfael was never going to surrender his private reservations about any reputed saint who could describe humankind as a mass of corruption and sin proceeding inevitably towards death, or one who could look upon the world, for all its imperfections, and find it irredeemably evil. Nor could he accept that the number of those predestined to salvation was fixed, limited and immutable, as Augustine proclaimed, nor indeed that the fate of any man was sealed and hopeless from his birth, or why not throw away all regard for others and rob and murder and lay waste, and indulge every anarchic appetite in this world, having nothing beyond to look forward to?   16(2)

St Augustine of Hippo was born in the fourth century in Numidia (Algeria) to a pagan father and a Christian mother. He suffered long and agonising inward conflict before being baptised a Christian in his early thirties. The most important of his many works are the Confessions *and the* City of God.

July

20th 'I've found that Saint Augustine went through many changes of mind over the years. You could take some of his early writings, and they say the very opposite of what he said in old age. That, and a dozen changes between. Cadfael, did you ever think what a waste it would be if you burned a man for what he believed at twenty, when what he might believe and write at forty would be hailed as the most blessed of holy writ?'

'That is the kind of argument to which the most of men never listen,' said Cadfael, 'otherwise they would baulk at taking any life.'

16(13)

21st Saint Augustine regarded the sin of Adam as perpetuated in all his heirs. It might be well to give a thought to what the sin of Adam truly was. Augustine held it to be the fleshly act between man and woman, and considered it the root and origin of all sin. There is here another disputable point. If this in every case is sin, how comes it that God instructed his first-made creatures to be fruitful and multiply and people the earth?

16(15)

22nd Earth is innocent. Only the use we make of it mars it.

17(2)

July

23rd He sat in his solitude and seriously considered whether a man was really better for reading anything at all, let alone these labyrinthine works of theology that served only to make the clear and bright seem muddied and dim, by clothing everything they touched in words obscure and shapeless as mist, far out of the comprehension of ordinary men, of whom the greater part of the human creation is composed. When he looked out from the cell window, at a narrow lancet of pale blue sky fretted with the tremor of leaves and feathered with a few wisps of bright white cloud, everything appeared to him radiant and simple again, within the grasp of even the meanest, and conferring benevolence impartially and joyously upon all.

16(10)

24th Do not strain after perfection.   8(1)

25th It is native to man to have an aim, and labour towards it. And God he knows, better than any, that grace and truth and uprightness are as good aims as any. What else is salvation? It is no bad thing to feel obliged to earn it, and not wait to be given it as alms to a beggar, unearned.

16(15)

July

26th 'Along the way a man lives a day at a time, and looks no further ahead than the next day, and no further behind than the day just passed. Now I see it whole, and it is wonderful.'

'But not all good,' said Cadfael. 'That couldn't be, we couldn't ask it. Remember the cold and the rain and the hunger at times, and losses by thieves now and then, and a few knocks from those who prey on travellers – oh, never tell me you met none! And the weariness, and the times when you fell ill, the bad food, the sour water, the stones of the road. You've met all that. Every man who travels that far across the world has met it all.'

'I do remember all that, but it is still wonderful.'

'Good! So it should be,' said Cadfael.   16(3)

Cadfael was talking to Elave, who, in 1143, had just returned to
Shrewsbury after a long pilgrimage to the Holy Land.

27th He reads, and he thinks about what he reads. He brought back more than silver pence from the Holy Land. An intelligent man's baggage on such a journey must be light, but in his mind he can accumulate a world.   16(10)

28th Words, words, I don't doubt they were spoken, but words can be interpreted many ways, and even a small doubt cast can alter the image.   16(6)

July

29th Cadfael's fragrant domain, dewy from the dawn and already warming into drunken sweetness in the rising sun, filled his senses with the kind of pleasure on which an ascetic church sometimes frowns, finding something uneasily sinful in pure delight. There were times when the young brother, who worked with him in this delectable field, felt that he ought to confess his joy among his sins, and meekly accept some appropriate penance. He was still very young, there were excuses to be found for him. Brother Cadfael had more sense, and no such scruples. The manifold gifts of God are there to be delighted in, to fall short of joy would be ingratitude.

4(1:1)

Blessed with humility and simplicity of nature, young Brother Mark worked for two years as Cadfael's assistant in the herb-gardens at Shrewsbury Abbey before going to Lichfield to study for the priesthood.

30th Saints have a right to suppose that their devotees mean what they say, and bestow gifts accordingly.   1(10)

31st A man cannot be in and out of a workshop saturated with years of harvesting herbs, and not carry the scent of them about in his garments.   12(9)

August

❀❖❀

August was high harvest time among the herbs, and all the medicines for the winter demanding Cadfael's care. 2(1)

August

1st (The First Day of St Peter's Fair)

No place like one of your greater fairs for exchanging news and views without being noticed, or laying plots and stratagems, or meeting someone you'd liefer not be seen meeting. Nowhere so solitary as in the middle of a market-place! 4(1:2)

2nd (The Second Day of St Peter's Fair)

Tongues wag more freely before the deaf man. 4(5:2)

3rd (The Third Day of St Peter's Fair)

The summer period of Saint Peter's fair was the chief populator of the abbey cells, since it could be relied upon to provide two happy drunken servants or lay brothers nightly, who slept off their excesses and accepted their modest fines and penances without rancour, thinking the game well worth the candle. 3(7)

August

4th Let us have some room for thought before we accuse or exonerate any man. And before all, let someone who knows his business make good sure that the man is out of reach of help, or we are *all* guilty of his death.   20(5)

5th Every untimely death, every man cut down in his vigour and strength without time for repentance and reparation, is one corpse too many.   2(12)

6th 'The dead are in God's hand,' said Cadfael. 'You may not wish them back.'   6(14)

August

7th Every man's fortune, and every woman's too, can be changed given a little thought, perseverance and cunning.   7(4)

8th We stand now where these faults and betrayals, from whatever source, have left us, and from where we stand we must proceed, we have no other choice. What is to be done *now*, to undo such ills as may be undone, is what we have to fathom. Let all be said with that in mind, and not revenges for things long past.   20(4)

9th As for what you have lost, it is lost only to this world.

13(1)

August

10th 'It was in the night, and I was cold, and I thought to myself, I wish the good God would send me a cloak to keep me warm! Brother, thought is also prayer! And no more than three days later God did indeed send me a cloak. You dropped it into my arms! How can I be at peace? The young man who owned this very coat gave me a groat that night, and asked me to say a prayer for him on the morrow, and so I did. But how if my first prayer made the second of none effect? How if I have prayed a man into his grave to get myself a cloak to wear?'

'Put all such thoughts out of your mind, friend,' said Cadfael firmly, 'for only the devil can have sent them. If God gave you the thing for which you wished, it was to save one morsel of good out of a great evil for which you are no way to blame. Surely your prayers for the former bearer are of aid even now to his soul. You need have no fears, his death is not at your door, and no sacrifice of yours could have saved him.'

2(11)

During the siege of Shrewsbury in 1138, the beggar, Lame Osbern,
saw a young man enter King Stephen's camp at around midnight, wearing
a cloak with a bronze dragon clasp at the neck. After the young man's corpse
had been found among the executed dead, Cadfael — by chance — gave
the cloak to Osbern as an act of charity.

August

11^{**th**} This open-eyed understanding and pity repelled him beyond hope. How dared a green, simple virgin, who had never become aware of his body but through his lameness and physical pain, recognise the fire when it scorched him, and respond only with compassion? No fear, no blame, and no uncertainty. Nor would he complain to confessor or superior. The brother went away with grief and desire burning in his bowels, and the remembered face of the woman clear and cruel before his mind's eyes. Prayer was no cure for the memory of her.   11(3)

Rejected by his wife, Urien tried to find solace by becoming a monk at Shrewsbury Abbey. Tormented by memories of the woman he still loved, Urien saw her remembered face in sixteen-year-old Brother Rhun and tried to find comfort in him. Despite his innocence, Rhun acted with candour: 'He did not snatch his hand away, but withdrew it very gently and kindly, and turned his fair head to look Urien full in the face with wide, wide-set eyes of the clearest blue-grey, with such comprehension and pity that the wound burned unbearably deep, corrosive with rage and shame. Urien took his hand away and turned aside from him.'

12^{**th**} The old in age and experience might well find a bitter flavour in viewing impossible fruit.   5(1)

August

13th He who has no scruple has always the advantage of those who keep the rule. 10(6)

✿❖✿

14th What is the use of mending a man, if he's to be broken within a few hours, past mending?'

'We were speaking of souls,' said Cadfael mildly, 'not mere bodies. And who knows but your touch with ointment and linen may have mended to better effect the one that lasts the longer? There's no arrow cleaves the soul. But there may be balm for it.' 4(4:4)

✿❖✿

15th The means of comfort and healing must not be used to kill. 3(9)

August

16^{**th**} It is our work to teach the young how to deal with the temptations of the world and the flesh, but certainly not our duty to subject them to such temptations. 13(2)

17^{**th**} Cadfael had still the crusader blood quick within him, he could not choose but awake and respond, however the truth had sunk below his dreams and hopes, all those years ago. Others, no less, had believed and trusted, no less to shudder and turn aside from much of what was done in the name of the Faith. 11(2)

August

18th Keep your lips locked among others. We are in the battle-
field in the abbey, as sure as in the town, our gates never
being closed to any. All manner of men rub shoulders here, and in
rough times some may try to buy favour with carrying tales. Some
may even be collectors of such tales for their living. Your thoughts are
safe in your head, best keep them there. 2(1)

19th Penitence is in the heart, not in the words spoken. 4(2:1)

20th 'We do the best we can with our lives!' And the worst,
Cadfael thought, with other men's lives, if we have power.
2(3)

August

21st Brother Cadfael had behaved himself extremely modestly and circumspectly these last days, strict to every scruple of the horarium, prompt in every service, trying, he admitted to himself ruefully, to deserve success, and disarm whatever disapproval the heavens might be harbouring against him. The end in view, he was certain, was not only good but vitally necessary, for the sake of the abbey and the church. But the means — he was less certain that the means were above reproach. But what can a man do, or a woman either, but use what comes to hand? 11(14)

22nd If he had missed Vespers, so be it. He valued and respected his duties, but if they clashed, he knew which way he must go. 2(4)

August

23rd We Welsh are not quick in respect to rank or riches, we do not doff and bow and scrape when any man flaunts himself before us. We are blunt and familiar even in praise. What we value we value in the heart.

1(3)

24th The disease of mortality is in us from the womb, from the day of our birth we are on the way to our death. What matters is how we conduct the journey.

8(11)

25th Which of us has never been guilty of some unworthiness that sorts very ill with what our friends know of us? Even with what we know, or think we know, of ourselves! I would not rule out any man from being capable once in his life of a gross infamy.

9(11)

August

26th No, I have had no regrets. But neither did I know what there might be worth regretting. And I have known those who did rebel, even wanting that knowledge. It may be they imagined a better world without than is possible in this life, and it may be that I lack that gift of imagination. Or it may be only that I was fortunate in finding work here within to my liking and within my scope, and have been too busy to repine. I would not change. But my choice would have been the same if I had grown to puberty here, and made my vows only when I was grown. I have cause to know that others would have chosen differently, had they been free. 8(1)

The abbot — while planning to abandon the custom of allowing young children to enter the monastery — asked Brother Edmund (who had entered at the tender age of four) whether he ever regretted not having experience of the world outside the abbey walls. After which, the abbot sought the views of Brother Cadfael, who had entered much later in life.

August

27th 'Brother Cadfael, what of you? You have ranged over much of the world, as far as the Holy Land, and borne arms. Your choice was made late and freely, and I do not think you have looked back. Was that gain, to have seen so much, and yet chosen this small hermitage?'

Cadfael found himself compelled to think before he spoke. He was by no means certain what the abbot wanted from him, but had no doubt whatever of his own indignant discomfort at the notion of a babe in arms being swaddled willy-nilly in the habit he himself had assumed willingly. 'I think it was gain,' he said at length, 'and more-over, a better gift I brought, flawed and dinted though it might be, than if I had come in my innocence. For I own freely that I had loved my life, and valued high the warriors I had known, and the noble places and great actions I had seen, and if I chose in my prime to renounce all these, and embrace this life of the cloister in preference to all other, then truly I think I paid the best compliment and homage I had to pay. And I cannot believe that anything I hold in my remembrance makes me less fit to profess this allegiance, but rather better fits me to serve as well as I may. Had I been given in infancy, I should have rebelled in manhood, wanting my rights. Free from childhood, I could well afford to sacrifice my rights when I came to wisdom.'

8(1)

August

28th 'However late the rosebuds come, they always bloom equally in the end.' It could have been a metaphor for the quality of a life. 13(1)

※❀※

29th The wholeness of his entranced peace, so far in excess of what most fallible human brothers could achieve, was a perpetual marvel. For him whatever God decreed and did, for him or to him, even to his grief and humiliation, even to his life, was done well. Martyrdom would not have changed his mind. 17(6)

※❀※

30th Did you ever feel that it might be better to let even ill alone, rather than let loose worse? 15(3)

August

31st A household of the indigent and helpless, men, women, even children, forsaken or left orphans, dappled by skin diseases, deformed by accident, leprosy and agues; and a leaven of reasonably healthy beggars who lacked only land, craft, a place in the orders, and the means to earn their bread.

In Wales, thought Cadfael, these things are better handled, not by charity but by blood-kinship. If a man belongs to a kinship, who can separate him from it? It acknowledges and sustains him, it will not let him be outcast or die of need. 8(7)

The leper-hospital of St Giles stood discreetly back from the road, about half a mile from Shrewsbury Abbey, and even further away from the town. Many of the brothers served a period of time there looking after the inmates — including Cadfael, who regularly supplied medicines.

September

September was again September, mellowed and fruitful after the summer heat and drought. Much of the abundant weight of fruit had fallen unplumped by reason of the dryness, but even so there would be harvest enough for thanksgiving.

11(14)

September

1st Once out of his bed, Cadfael had lost the fine art of being idle. He filled in the time until Prime with some work among the herbs, and some early watering while the sun was still climbing, round and dull gold behind its veil of haze. These functions his hands and eyes could take care of, while his mind was free to fret and speculate over the complicated fortunes of people for whom he had formed a strong affection.   11(10)

❊❖❊

2nd After every extreme the seasons righted themselves, and won back the half at least of what was lost. So might the seasons of men right themselves, with a little help by way of rain from heaven.   11(14)

❊❖❊

3rd 'All which,' said Cadfael cheerfully. 'God knows, and needs not to be told.'   4(2:1)

September

4th All about him, in the mid hours of the night, lightnings flared and instantly died again into blackness. And all in absolute silence, with nowhere any murmur of thunder to break the leaden hush. Forewarnings of the wrath of God, or of his inscrutable mercies.

11(11)

5th As for haste, it's neither you nor I that hold the measure. Death will come when it will come. Until then, every day is of consequence, the last no less than the first.

11(2)

6th Brother Cadfael's mind was firmly upon growth, rather than destruction and war.

2(1)

September

7th 'I have seen death in many shapes,' said Brother Cadfael. 'I've been soldier and sailor in my time; in the east, in the Crusade, and for ten years after Jerusalem fell. I've seen men killed in battle. Come to that, I've killed men in battle. I never took joy in it, that I can remember, but I never drew back from it, either, having made my vows.' 8(2)

8th Cadfael, whose two broad feet had always been solidly planted on earth, even when he took his convinced decision to come into harbour for the rest of a long life, had considerable sympathy with the ardent young, who overdo everything, and take wing at a line of verse or a snatch of music. Some who thus take fire burn to the day of their death, and set light to many others, leaving a trail of radiance to generations to come. Other fires sink for want of fuel, but do no harm to any. 8(1)

9th Praise God! We are here! 6(4)

September

10th Do you think that small children know when they are only second best? I think he knew it early. He was different even to look at, but that was the least part. I think he always went the opposing way, whatever they wished upon him. If his father said white, he said black; wherever they tried to turn him, he dug in his heels hard and wouldn't budge. He couldn't help learning, because he was sharp and curious, so he grew lettered, but when he knew they wanted him a clerk, he went after all manner of low company, and flouted his father every way. He's always been jealous of his elder brother, but always worshipped him. He flouts his father purposely, because he knows he's loved less, and that grieves him bitterly, and yet he can't hate his brother for being loved more. 8(6)

Meriet Aspley idolised his elder brother, Nigel; yet was jealous of the fact that Nigel was his father's favourite son. His response was to rebel.

11th He made his choice. I was taught to think it the wrong one, but at least he stood by it to the end. His father might have been angry with him, but he would not have had to be ashamed.

2(4)

September

12th He is by nature honest and sweet clean through, whatever manner of wreck he and other people and ill circumstances may have made of his life. I only wish he were happier. I should like to hear him laugh. 8(7)

13th As the world usually goes, he probably has a mind that looks no further ahead or behind than the length of his own fine eyelashes. But I grant you he's a pleasure to look at. Yet the mind lasts longer. Be glad you have one that will wear well. 4(1:1)

14th Beauty is a very healing thing. 5(1)

September

15th Cadfael, like a fisherman with a shy and tricky bite on his line, went on paying out small-talk, easing suspicion, engaging interest, exposing, as he did not often do, the past years of his own experience. The silence favoured by the Order ought not to be allowed to stand in the way of its greater aims, where a soul was tormenting itself on the borders of conviction. A garrulous old brother, harking back to an adventurous past, ranging half the known world – what could be more harmless, or more disarming?   8(2)

16th In the end I came home, because it was home and I felt the need of it.   8(2)

17th Cadfael turned back into his workshop, and barred the door against all the rest of the world. It was very quiet in there, and very dim with the darkness of the timber walls and the faint blue smoke from the brazier. A home within a home to him now, and all he wanted.   3(11)

September

18th The boys, by the abbot's orders separated from their elders, slept in a small room at the end of the dortoir, and a trusted brother occupied the cell that shielded their private place. He knew and understood the unforeseen dangers that lurked in ambush for celibate souls, however innocent. 8(2)

19th You must not take to yourself more than your due. What you yourself did, that you may rue, and confess, and do penance for, to your soul's content, but you may not lift another man's sins from his shoulders, or usurp God's right to be the only judge. 6(8)

20th My wants are simple, I make no complaint. I never doubt time will bring me my due. First to earn it. 7(8)

Autumn

Autumn was a good time, since there was digging to be done, to make the cleared ground ready for the operation of the frosts to come.   5(2)

21st There are seasons of love. Theirs had passed beyond the storms of spring and the heat of summer into the golden calm of the first autumn days, before the leaves begin to fall. She looked as he looked, confirmed and invulnerable in the peace of the spirit. Henceforth presence was unnecessary, and passion irrelevant. They were eased of the past, and both of them had work to do for the future, all the more eagerly and thoroughly for knowing, each of them, that the other lived and laboured in the same vineyard. 15(14)

Deceived into believing that his teenage lover, Bertrade de Clary (together with the child she carried, his child), was dead, and that he was largely responsible, Haluin forsook the world and entered Shrewsbury Abbey as a novice. Years later, having endured terrible remorse, guilt and self-punishment for his action, Haluin discovered — to his wonder and joy — that Bertrade was alive and well, living as Sister Benedicta at Farewell Abbey. Their child, also, had not died, but had grown into a beautiful woman, the image of her mother.

September

22nd He had been given, for his sins, the most cheerful, guileless, heedless and handless of cherubs, eternally hopeful, never chastened, a raw novice of nineteen fixed for ever at the age of a happy child of twelve. His fingers were all thumbs, but his zest and confidence were absolute. Cadfael liked him, as he was infuriated by him, out of all measure, and gloomily made large allowance for the damage the lad was almost certain to do whenever left to follow instructions unsupervised. Still, he had virtues, besides his sweetness of nature. For rough digging, the chief challenge of autumn, he had no peer, he plunged into it with the vigour others devoted to prayer, and turned the loam with a love and fellow-feeling Cadfael could not but welcome. Only keep him from planting what he dug! He had black fingers!

5(1)

Brother Oswin replaced Brother Mark as Cadfael's assistant in the herb-gardens at Shrewsbury Abbey. Despite his glowing enthusiasm, sweetness of nature and exuberant energy, he often left a trail of havoc behind him.

September

23rd Surely the very motions she had made in his presence, so slight and so conscious, had been made in the knowledge that he was well aware of them, cobweb threads to entrammel one more unlikely fly. He was careful not to look back, for it had dawned on him that she would confidently expect him to.　　8(5)

❈◈❈

24th Swathed warmly in a fine blue cloak that concealed all but the rosy oval of her face, she still knew how to radiate beauty, and oh, she knew, how well she knew, that she had at least forty pairs of innocent male eyes upon her, marvelling at what strange delights were withheld from them. Women of all ages, practical and purposeful, went in and out regularly at these gates, with complaint, appeal, request and gift, and made no stir and asked no tribute. She came armed in knowledge of her power, and delighted in the disquiet she brought with her. There would be some strange dreams among the novices.　　8(10)

September

25th 'Oh, Brother Cadfael, how does it come that a brother of this house can know far too much about us women!'

'As I suppose,' said Cadfael cautiously, 'I was born of one, like the rest of us. Even abbots and archbishops come into the world the same way.'

4(1:1)

26th Her reserves of money might now be far longer than her reserves of peace of mind were likely to be; she could afford to buy herself a little consolation, and prayers are never wasted.

4(2:1)

27th Salvation comes from strange places and unexpected friends.

12(12)

September

28th Child, as long as you live and breathe you will not have done with this world. We within the pale live in the same world as all poor souls without.   9(8)

✠❖✠

29th There are medicines to soothe a too-fevered mind. Brother Cadfael has such. But they are aids that should be used only in grave need, while you seek better cures in prayer, and in the mastery of yourself.   8(2)

✠❖✠

30th What is done matters, but what is yet to do matters far more.   9(15)

October

❦

The soft October days slid away tranquilly one after another, in dim, misty dawns, noon-days bright but veiled, and moist green twilights magically still. 14(2)

October

1st We have not the tools by which to measure values concerning the soul. That is God's business. Rather it behoves us to live every day as though it were our last, to the full of such truth and kindness as is within us, and to lie down every night as though the next day were to be our first, and a new and pure beginning.   12(11)

2nd It may well be that our justice sees as in a mirror image, left where right should be, evil reflected back as good, good as evil, your angel as her devil. But God's justice, if it makes no haste, makes no mistakes.   17(14)

3rd Even God, when he intends mercy, needs tools to his hand.   9(15)

October

4th Fear for yourself crushes and compresses you from without, but fear for another is a monster, a ravenous rat gnawing within, eating out your heart.

7(5)

5th We are born of the fathers we deserve, and they engender the sons they deserve. We are our own penance and theirs. The first murderous warfare in the world, we are told, was between two brothers, but the longest and the bitterest is between fathers and sons.

20(8)

6th As for old age, he had not yet begun to think about it; no doubt it had its own alleviations.

4(3:1)

October

7th There are secrets which should be buried beyond discovery, things, even people, lost beyond finding, for their own sake, for all our sakes.   11(10)

❋❖❋

8th In the shrouded anonymity of dark cloak and hood, and the cloth veil that hid even the faces of those worse disfigured, men and women, old and young, seemed to go secretly and alone through the remnant of life left to them. No gender, no age, no colouring, no country, no creed: all living ghosts, known only to their maker. But no, it was not so. By gait, by voice, by stature, by a thousand infinitesimal foibles of character and kind that pierced through the disguise, they emerged every one unique.   5(1)

October

9th Beyond a certain strength treatment cannot go. Beyond that there is only one cure, and we are forbidden to resort to that. None the less, I did consider how to die. Mortal sin, Father, I knew it, yet I did consider. I foresaw a time when the load would become more than even I could bear, and I wished to have some small thing about me, a little vial of deliverance, a promise of peace, perhaps never to use, only to keep as a talisman, the very touch of it consolation to me that at the worst . . . at the last extreme, there was left to me a way of escape. To know that was to go on enduring.   17(14)

Suffering from a long debilitating illness, Donata Blount found comfort in possessing a small vial of deadly poisonous hemlock.

10th After fourscore years I wonder if death should be accounted troublous.   7(11)

11th Distant death is one thing, its actual presence quite another.   14(2)

October

12th No need to pretend that violence and danger and cruelty do not exist, and men do not die. 6(4)

❖

13th Cadfael said nothing; there was nothing reassuring or consoling to be said. Such things were the commonplace of marriage where there were lands and wealth and powerful alliances to be gained, and small say the brides – or often enough the young bridegrooms – had in the disposal of their persons. There might even be brides who could see shrewdly enough the advantages of marrying men old enough to be their grandsires, where there was material good to be gained, since death might very soon relieve them of their husbands but leave them their dower and the status of their widowhood, and with some luck and a deal of cleverness they might manage to make a second match more to their liking. 5(1)

Cadfael was pondering an exclamation made by Brother Mark about the arranged marriage of a young girl to a man old enough to be her grandfather: 'So small, and so young! And did you see her face – how sad! This is not with her will!'

October

14th This woman had subsided placidly into middle age, had let the wrinkles form in her face and neck without disguise, and the grey invade her brown hair. Brisk and lively she still was, and would always be, sure of herself, feeling no need to be or seem other than she was.

5(8)

15th Many things, used wrongly, or used in excess, can kill a man. Even wine, if you take enough of it. Even wholesome food, if you devour it beyond reason.

3(1)

October

16th It behoves a man to look within himself, and turn to the best dedication possible those endowments he has from his Maker. 17(4)

17th Cadfael looked back to the turning-point of his life, many years past. After all manner of journeying, fighting, endurance of heat and cold and hardship, after the pleasures and the pains of experience, the sudden irresistible longing to turn about and withdraw into quietness remained a mystery. Not a retreat, certainly. Rather an emergence into light and certainty. 17(1)

October

18th He never could explain it or describe it. All he could say was that he had had a revelation of God, and had turned where he was pointed, and come where he was called. It happens.

17(1)

✤✤✤

19th A pity, a great pity there should be so much hurrying on of death, when it's bound to reach every man in its own good time.

14(6)

✤✤✤

20th There is no haste. For the present take your full place here among us. Rest some days, pray constantly for guidance, have faith that it will be granted, and then choose. For the choice must be yours, let no one take it from you.

17(4)

October

21ˢᵗ Bleak necessity, to be forced to wish for any man's death, but this one has been the death of so many others, souls humble and defenceless, and by such abominable means, I could find it in me to offer prayers for his ending, as a needful mercy to his neighbours. How else can there ever be peace and good husbandry in those desolated lands? 17(9)

Geoffrey de Mandeville, Earl of Essex, took revenge on King Stephen's confiscation of his offices and castles by ruthlessly killing and torturing the inhabitants of the Cambridgeshire Fens. He converted Ramsey Abbey into an island fortress from which he plundered the surrounding countryside. He was struck in the head by an arrow in August 1144 and died of the wound the following month.

22ⁿᵈ There will always be the haters among us. 17(6)

23ʳᵈ Among humankind all things are possible. 7(11)

October

24th So all we need, Cadfael thought, is a little ingenuity in dealing with his conscience, and a little manipulating of truth in gradually laying the case to rest. Given time, gossip will tire of the affair, and turn to the next small crisis or scandal around the town, and they will forget at last that their curiosity was never satisfied, and no culprit ever brought to book. And there, he realised, was where he came into headlong collision with his own unsatisfied desire to have truth, if not set out before the public eye, at least unearthed, recognised and acknowledged. How, otherwise, could there be real reconciliation with life and death and the ordinances of God?

17(13)

Sulien Blount confessed to a murder he did not commit to protect his father, whom he wrongly thought was guilty of the crime. When the facts were revealed, Sulien was guilty of nothing but suppressing the truth; his father was guilty of secretly burying the body trying to protect his family name. The victim died by her own hand, drinking a draught of poison after making the wrong choice in a life or death gamble. As the father was now dead, killed in battle, Cadfael felt there was little point in making the facts public.

October

25th One nobility is kin to another. There are alliances that cross the blood-line of families, the borders of countries, even the impassable divide of religion.   5(11)

26th God fixes the term, not men, not kings, not judges. A man must be prepared to face life, as well as death, there's no escape from either.   9(15)

27th He has gone far along a difficult road who has come to the point of seeing that deprivation, pain and disability are of no consequence at all, beside the inward conviction of grace, and the secret peace of the soul. An acceptance which can only be made for a man's own self, never for any other.   10(4)

October

28th God's vision is clearer than mine, he may both see a way out of this tangle and open my eyes to it when the time is ripe. There's a path through every forest, and a safe passage somewhere through every marsh, it needs only the finding. 11(10)

29th Truth, like the burgeoning of a bulb under the soil, however deeply sown, will make its way to the light.

17(10)

October

30th At the end of Vespers Cadfael lingered in his stall, letting the procession of brothers and novices file out into the cloister without him. The office had its beauty and consolation, but the echoes of the music had all died away, and to be here alone in this evening hour had a special beneficence, whether because of the soft, dove-coloured light or the sense of enlargement that seemed to swell the soul to inhabit and fill the last arches of the vault, as a single drop of water becomes the ocean into which it falls. There was no better time for profound prayer, and Cadfael felt the need of it.   14(9)

October

31st 'I have transgressed against my vocation,' said Cadfael, at once solaced and saddened by the season and the hour. 'I know it. I undertook the monastic life, but now I am not sure I could support it without you, without these stolen excursions outside the walls. For so they are. True, I am often sent upon legitimate labours here without, but also I steal, I take more than is my due by right. Worse, I do not repent me! Do you suppose there is room within the bounds of grace for one who has set his hand to the plough, and every little while abandons his furrow to turn back among the sheep and lambs?'

'I think the sheep and lambs might think so. He would have their prayers. Even the black sheep and the grey, like some you've argued for against God and me in your time.'

'There are very few all black,' said Cadfael. 'Dappled, perhaps. Most of us have a few mottles about us. As well, maybe, it makes for a more tolerant judgement of the rest of God's creatures. But I have sinned, and most of all in relishing my sin. I shall do penance by biding dutifully within the walls through the winter, unless I'm sent forth, and then I'll make haste with my task and hurry back.'

'Until the next waif stumbles across your path. And when is this penance to begin?'

'Tomorrow,' said Cadfael. 'If God wills, tomorrow.'   14(13)

Cadfael often confided in his friend Hugh Beringar, unburdening his
innermost thoughts and feelings over a shared flask of wine inside
his herb-scented workshop.

November

November, and the season for markets and fairs over, but the weather still fairly mild and dry.   17(7)

November

1st He had never been quite so acutely aware of the particular quality and function of November, its ripeness and its hushed sadness. The year proceeds not in a straight line through the seasons, but in a circle that brings the world and man back to the dimness and mystery in which both began, and out of which a new seed-time and a new generation are about to begin. Old men, thought Cadfael, believe in that new beginning, but experience only the ending. It may be that God is reminding me that I am approaching my November. Well, why regret it? November has beauty, has seen the harvest into the barns, even laid by next year's seed. No need to fret about not being allowed to stay and sow it, someone else will do that. So go contentedly into the earth with the moist, gentle, skeletal leaves, worn to cobweb fragility, like the skins of very old men, that bruise and stain at the mere brushing of the breeze, and flower into brown blotches as the leaves into rotting gold. The colours of late autumn are the colours of the sunset: the farewell of the year and the farewell of the day. And of the life of man? Well, if it ends in a flourish of gold, that is no bad ending. 20(1)

November

2nd It is only that the step from perfectly ordinary things into the miraculous seems to me so small, almost accidental, that I wonder why it astonishes you at all, or why you trouble to reason about it. If it were reasonable it could not be miraculous, could it?

19(10)

***

3rd How can you fly from beings who are everywhere and see everything?

1(10)

***

4th I think there are some who live on a knife-edge in the soul, and at times are driven to hurl themselves into the air, at the mercy of heaven or hell which way to fall.

1(7)

November

5th In the vast, dim quiet of the church Cadfael made amicable obeisance to the altar of Saint Winifred, as to an intimate but revered friend, but for once hesitated to burden her with a charge for another man. So the only prayer he made to her was made without words, in the heart, offering affection in a gush of tenderness like the smoke of incense. She had forgiven him so much, and never shut him out. And this same year she had suffered flood and peril and contention, and come back safely to a deserved rest. Why disturb its sweetness with a trouble which belonged all to himself? So he took his problem rather to the high altar, directly to the source of all strength, all power, all faithfulness, and for once he was not content to kneel, but prostrated himself in a cross on the cold flags, like an offender presenting his propitiatory body at the end of penance, though the offence he contemplated was not yet committed, and with great mercy and understanding on his superior's part might not be necessary. Nevertheless, he professed his intent now, in stark honesty, and besought rather comprehension than forgiveness. With his forehead chill against the stone he discarded words to present his compulsion, and let thoughts express the need that found him lucid but inarticulate. This I must do, whether with a blessing or a ban. For whether I am blessed or banned is of no consequence, provided what I have to do is done well.   20(I)

In 1145, after twenty-five years at Shrewsbury Abbey, Cadfael planned to betray his vows and discard his vocation in order to find his son, Olivier de Bretagne, who had been imprisoned in some unknown location.

November

6th The old man's dying was painless and feather-light, all the substance of his once sharp and vigorous mind gone on before; but it was slow. The fading candle flame did not flicker, only dimmed in perfect stillness second by second, so mysteriously that they missed the moment when the last spark withdrew, and only knew he was gone when they began to realise that the prints of age were smoothing themselves out gently from his face.

'A blessed death as ever I saw! I wonder will God deal as gently with me, when my time comes!' 14(4)

The person who died was 'an old, retired brother' of Shrewsbury Abbey.

7th Pain is as good a dragon to fight as any in this world. 10(5)

November

8th He forgot her as soon as she was out of sight. He knew about these affairs. If you were only ten years old they didn't, for some reason, make you live with your wife, not until you were grown up. While she remained under the same roof with you, you would be expected to be civil to her, perhaps even attentive, but then she would go back with her father to her own home until you were thought to be old enough to share your bed and household with her. Now that he began to think seriously about it, it seemed to him that there were no privileges at all attached to being married. 14(10)

Ten-year-old Richard Ludel was forced to marry an heiress over twice his age, so that his grandmother could gain possession of two neighbouring manors.

9th Traffic with the world is laid upon us for chastening, and for the testing of our vocation. The grace of God is not endangered by the follies or the wickedness of men. 5(11)

10th There is no need for me to say it, since you know it yourself. 7(9)

November

11th Brother Cadfael was standing in the middle of his walled herb-garden, looking pensively about him at the autumnal visage of his pleasance, where all things grew gaunt, wiry and sombre. Most of the leaves were fallen, the stems dark and clenched like fleshless fingers holding fast to the remnant of the summer, all the fragrances gathered into one scent of age and decline, still sweet, but with the damp, rotting sweetness of harvest over and decay setting in. It was not yet very cold, the mild melancholy of November still had lingering gold in it, in falling leaves and slanting amber light. All the apples were in the loft, all the corn milled, the hay long stacked, the sheep turned into the stubble fields. A time to pause, to look round, to make sure nothing had been neglected, no fence unrepaired, against the winter.

20(1)

November

12th 'I took my vows in good faith,' said Cadfael, 'not then knowing that there was in the world a being for whose very existence I was responsible. From all other ties my vows absolved me. All other personal relationships my vows severed. Not this one! Whether I would have resigned the world if I had known it contained my living seed, that I cannot answer, nor may you hazard at an answer. But he lives, and it was I engendered him. He suffered captivity and I am free. He may be in peril, and I am safe. Father, can the creator forsake the least of his creatures? Can a man turn away from his own imperilled blood? Is not procreation itself the undertaking of a sacred and inviolable vow? Knowing or unknowing, before I was a brother I was a father.'   20(1)

Departing from the Holy Land by way of Antioch in 1113, Cadfael was unaware that he had left his lover, Mariam, a Saracen widow, pregnant with their illegitimate child. He did not know that he was a father until some twenty-six years later, by which time he had been a monk for almost twenty years.

❋❖❋

13th What God imposed, no doubt for his own good reasons, for reasons as good he has lifted away.   5(11)

November

14th Your own man, the abbot had said, no longer any man of mine. Vows abandoned, brothers forsaken, heaven discarded. The first need was to recognise that it had happened, the second to accept it. After that Cadfael could ride on composedly, and be his own man, as for the former half of his life he had been, and only rarely felt a need beyond, until he found community and completion in surrendering himself. Life could and must be lived on those same terms for this while, perhaps for all the while remaining. So by that time he could look about him again, pay attention to the way, and turn his mind to the task that lay before him. 20(6)

In search of the whereabouts of his son, taken prisoner at Faringdon, Brother Cadfael was given leave to attend the council at Coventry in November 1145. To go further or delay further meant that he went without the abbot's leave or blessing. Cadfael chose not to return to Shrewsbury, but to head south into the Cotswolds to find his son.

November

15th In entering any other church but his own Cadfael missed, for one moment, the small stone altar and the chased reliquary where Saint Winifred was not, and yet was. Just to set eyes on it was to kindle a little living fire within his heart. Here he must forgo that particular consolation, and submit to an unfamiliar benediction. Nevertheless, there was an answer here for every need. 20(4)

16th The very act of kneeling in solitude, in the chill and austerity of stone, and saying the familiar words almost silently before the altar, brought him more of comfort and reassurance than he had dared to expect. If grace was not close to him, why should he rise from his knees so cleansed of the doubts and anxieties of the day, and clouded by no least shadow of the morrow's uncertainties? 20(9)

November

17th It is not enough to say that a thing is so because of one fragment of knowledge, even so clear as a confession, and put away out of sight those other things known, because they cannot be explained. An answer to a matter of life and death must be an answer that explains all. 6(14)

18th I heard many words. And even the silences between them were not altogether inarticulate. 15(5)

19th All the more to be desired was this order and tranquillity within the pale, where the battle of heaven and hell was fought without bloodshed, with the weapons of the mind and the soul. 20(16)

November

20th There is much to be said for being an island off the main. Invasions, curses and plagues are slower to reach you, and arrive so weakened as to be almost exhausted beforehand. Yet even distance may not always be a perfect defence.   16(10)

21st Those who had survived this upheaval to gain, instead of loss, might safely be left to draw breath and think in peace, before they must encounter and come to new terms. And those who had lost must have time to lick their wounds.   8(13)

November

22nd Where most men are still dreaming of total victory, the few who would be content with an economical compromise carry no weight. And yet at the last, this was the way it must go, there could be no other ending. Neither side could ever win, neither side lose. 20(4)

❦

23rd A pity there should have to be factions, and decent men fighting one another, and all of them convinced they have the right of it. 14(9)

❦

24th Decent, quiet men were the backbone of any community, to be respected and valued beyond those who made the biggest commotion and the most noise in the world. 13(2)

November

25th There are more ways than one of getting into a castle, Cadfael reasoned. The simplest of all, for a lone man without an army or any means of compulsion, is to ride up to the gate and ask to be let in. 20(7)

26th Nothing could now be done before dawn. Not by men. But God, after all, knew where the lost might be found, and it would do no harm to put in a word in that quarter, and admit the inadequacy of human effort. 6(8)

27th He had time, now, to kneel and wait, having busied himself thus far in anxious efforts like a man struggling up a mountain, when he knew there was a force that could make the mountain bow. 4(4:3)

November

28th Beware how you pass judgement on your superiors, at least until you know how to put yourself in their place and see from their view. 3(1)

29th Afterwards, of course, there were plenty of wiseacres pregnant with hindsight, listing portents, talking darkly of omens, brazenly asserting that they had told everyone so. After every shock and reverse, such late experts proliferate. 8(1)

30th It was good to put all worries aside and listen with good heart to the lives of saints who had shrugged off the cares of the world to let in the promises of a world beyond, and viewed earthly justice as no more than a futile shadow-play obscuring the absolute justice of heaven, for which no man need wait longer than the life-span of mortality. 9(8)

December

❦❖❧

ecember came in with heavy skies and dark, brief days that sagged upon the rooftrees and lay like oppressive hands upon the heart. 15(1)

December

1st It is a time for quietness and prayer. Death is present with us every day of our lives, it behoves us to take note of its nearness, not as a threat, but as our common experience on the way to grace. There is no more to be said. It is better to accept the will of God, and be silent.

5(5)

2nd Official justice does not dig deep, but regards what comes readily to the surface, and draws conclusions accordingly. A nagging doubt now and then is the price it pays for speedy order and a quiet land.

1(7)

December

3rd Chroniclers can edit names out as easily as visionaries can noise them abroad. 1(8)

❦

4th I grow old in experience of wonders, some of which turn out to fall somewhat short of their promise. I know of human deception, not always deliberate, for sometimes the deceiver is himself deceived. If saints have power, so have demons. 10(10)

❦

5th The urgent need came over him to recommit his own baffled endeavours to eyes that saw everything, and a power that could open all doors. 4(4:3)

December

6th Stranger things have happened in this strangest, most harrowing and most wonderful of worlds! 5(11)

❦❖❧

7th 'What I feel,' said Cadfael, 'when the divines begin talking doctrine, is that God speaks all languages, and whatever is said to him or of him in any tongue will need no interpreter.' 16(3)

December

8th 'Go where you were sent, bear what you were condemned to bear, and look for the meaning,' said Cadfael. 'For so must we all.'

10(14)

※◇※

9th He may be the one of his kind who does what his kind does not do. There is always one.

9(8)

※◇※

10th In our various degrees, we are all sinners. To acknowledge and accept that load is good. Perhaps even to acknowledge and accept it and not entertain either shame or regret may also be required of us. If we find we must still say: Yes, I would do the same again, we are making a judgement others may condemn. But how do we know that God will condemn it? His judgements are inscrutable.

20(16)

December

11th If the sin is one which, with all our will to do right, we cannot regret, can it truly be a sin? It was too deep for him. He wrestled with it night after night until from very weariness sleep came. In the end there is nothing to be done but to state clearly what has been done, without shame or regret, and say: Here I am, and this is what I am. Now deal with me as you see fit. That is your right. Mine is to stand by the act, and pay the price. You do what you must do, and pay for it. So in the end all things are simple.   20(16)

12th What Cadfael did not regret, he found grave difficulty in remembering to confess.   8(2)

13th Love in ignorance squanders what love, informed, crowds and overfills with tokens of eternity.   11(10)

December

14th I do not understand, thought Cadfael, but there is no need that I should. I trust, I respect and I love. Yet I have abandoned and left behind me what most I trust, respect and love, and whether I can ever get back to it again is more than I know. The assay is all.

20(14)

15th Those who want a door to close behind them must be either escaping into the world within or from the world without. There is a difference. But do you know a way of telling one from the other?

8(1)

16th You cannot surrender what you do not possess.

20(4)

173

December

17th Cadfael lay down on his face, close, close, his overlong hair brushing the shallow step up into the choir, his brow against the chill of the tiles, the absurd bristles of his unshaven tonsure prickly as thorns. His arms he spread wide, clasping the uneven edges of the patterned paving as drowning men hold fast to drifting weed. He prayed without coherent words, for all those caught between right and expedient, between duty and conscience, between the affections of earth and the abnegations of heaven. He did not sleep; but something short of a dream came into his alert and wakeful mind some while before dawn, as though the sun was rising before its hour, a warmth like a May morning full of blown hawthorn blossoms, and a girl, Saint Winifred, primrose-fair and unshorn, walking barefoot through the meadow grass, and smiling. He could not, or would not, go to her in her own altar within the choir, unabsolved as he was, but for a moment he had the lovely illusion that she had risen and was coming to him. Her white foot was on the very step beside his head, and she was stooping to touch him with her white hand, when the little bell in the dortoir rang to rouse the brothers for Prime.

20(16)

After abandoning his vows to go in search of his son, Cadfael returned to Shrewsbury Abbey to face the consequences of his actions: 'asking nothing, promising nothing, repenting nothing'.

December

18th A new man comes unmeasured and uneasy into a place not yet mellowed to him, and must be given time to breathe, and listen to the breathing of others. 12(2)

19th No need to rush at it, or you'll be in a muck sweat before you've done a dozen rows. What you must do is set an even pace, get a rhythm into it, and you can go on all day, the spade will keep time for you. Sing to it if you have breath enough, or hum with it and save your breath. You'll be surprised how the rows will multiply. There's an art in every labour. 12(2)

20th God direct all. It is, after all, a way he has. 4(5:4)

175

Winter

The winter had not yet begun to bite hard. The weather-wise foretold that there was bitter cold in store, heavy snows and hard prolonged frosts. 6(1)

❀❖❀

21ˢᵗ While you live, there is no way of escape from your part in humanity. 9(8)

❀❖❀

22ⁿᵈ Innocence is an infinitely fragile thing and thought can sometimes injure, even destroy it. 9(15)

December

23rd With the approach of Christmas it was quite usual for many of the merchants of Shrewsbury, and the lords of many small manors close by, to give a guilty thought to the welfare of their souls, and their standing as devout and ostentatious Christians, and to see small ways of acquiring merit, preferably as economically as possible. Some, of course, were selective in their giving, and made sure that their alms reached abbot or prior, on the assumption that his prayers might avail them more than those of the humbler brothers.

3(2)

(The Eve of the Nativity)

24th It's the nature of things that those who gather in great numbers for the feasts of the church should also disperse again to their various duties afterwards. Still, they need not all go away unchanged.

10(4)

December

25th   (The Day of the Nativity)

Cadfael had returned to the church after Prime to replenish the perfumed oil in the lamp on Saint Winifred's altar. The inquisitive skills which might have been frowned upon if they had been employed to make scents for women's vanity became permissible and even praiseworthy when used as an act of worship. It pleased him to think that the lady must take delight in being so served, for virgin saint though she might be, she was a woman, and in her youth had been a beautiful and desirable one.   12(8)

26th When choir monks and secular congregation met for worship together, the separation between them seemed accentuated rather than softened. We here, you out there, thought Brother Cadfael, and yet we are all like flesh, and our souls subject to the same final judgement.   12(11)

December

27th The dimness of the light, the solidity of the enclosing shadows, the muted voices, the absence of lay worshippers, all contributed to his sense of being enfolded in a sealed haven, where all those who shared in it were his own flesh and blood and spirit, responsible for him as he for them, even some for whom, in the active and arduous day, he could feel no love, and pretended none. The burden of his vows became also his privilege, and the night's first worship was the fuel of the next day's energy.   4(3:2)

28th Live, amend, in your dealings with sinners remember your own frailty, and in your dealings with the innocent, respect and use your own strength in their service. Do as well as you can, and leave the rest to God, and how much more can saints do?   3(10)

December

29th It's no blame to men if they try to put into their own artefacts all the colours and shapes God put into his.

4(1:1)

30th He stirred and sighed for the follies of men, and the presumptuous solemnity of the arrangements they made for lives they would never live.

11(4)

31st Life goes not in a straight line, but in a circle. The first half we spend venturing as far as the world's end from home and kin and stillness, and the latter half brings us back by roundabout ways but surely, to that state from which we set out.

18(4)